MIRROR TWIN

Also by Lynn Hightower

The Junie Lagarde Novels

THE BEAUTIFUL RISK *
SPIES IN PLAIN SIGHT *

The Enlightenment Project Novels

THE ENLIGHTENMENT PROJECT *
THE HUNTING DARK *

Novels

HIGH WATER
THE PIPER *
EVEN IN DARKNESS *

The Sonora Blair Series

EYESHOT
FLASHPOINT
NO GOOD DEED
THE DEBT COLLECTOR

The David Silver Series

ALIEN BLUES
ALIEN EYES
ALIEN HEAT
ALIEN RITES

The Lena Padget Series

SATAN'S LAMBS
FORTUNES OF THE DEAD
WHEN SECRETS DIE

**available from Severn House*

MIRROR TWIN

Lynn Hightower

First world edition published in Great Britain and the USA in 2026
by Severn House, an imprint of Canongate Books Ltd,
14 High Street, Edinburgh EH1 1TE.

severnhouse.com

Cover and jacket design by dholmesgraphic

British Library Cataloguing-in-Publication Data
A CIP catalogue record for this title is available from the British Library.

ISBN-13: 978-1-4483-1396-9 (cased)
ISBN-13: 978-1-4483-1899-5 (paper)
ISBN-13: 978-1-4483-1397-6 (e-book)

All Severn House titles are printed on acid-free paper.

Typeset by Palimpsest Book Production Ltd., Falkirk, Stirlingshire, Scotland.
Printed and bound in Great Britain by TJ Books, Padstow, Cornwall.

The manufacturer's authorised representative in the EU for product safety is Authorised Rep Compliance Ltd, 71 Lower Baggot Street, Dublin D02 P593 Ireland (arccompliance.com)

Praise for Lynn Hightower

"[A] spooky, suspenseful masterpiece . . .
Super-recommended!"
Lee Child on *The Enlightenment Project*

"Readers will compulsively turn pages to see how it all ends"
Publishers Weekly Starred Review of
The Enlightenment Project

"This taut psychological page-turner has a gripping, tightly woven plot and is jam-packed with head-spinning twists and an overwhelming sense of menace that will keep readers riveted"
Booklist on *Even in Darkness*

"Psychologically compelling"
Kirkus Reviews on *Even in Darkness*

"Fast pacing, a strong and sympathetic main character, and a genuinely frightening supernatural being keep the pages turning in this ghostly thriller"
Booklist on *The Piper*

"A stand-alone nightmare that will keep you awake till the last page and maybe even afterward"
Kirkus Reviews on *The Piper*

About the author

Lynn Hightower is the internationally bestselling author of numerous thriller and horror novels, including the Sonora Blair Mysteries, the Lena Padget Mysteries, the Enlightenment Project Novels, and the Junie Lagarde Novels. She has won the Shamus Award for Best First Private Eye novel, and a WHSmith Fresh Talent Award. She is published widely, including in France, Germany, Italy, and Japan.

She loves slow horses, big dogs, opinionated cats, and tiny sports cars. She has a German Shepherd who likes to be sung to, and she loves to curl up and write in any French village that will have her (the smaller the better, so she doesn't get lost).

www.lynnhightower.com

For Leah, my beloved German Shepherd.
Nous vivons vite.

ONE

I left in darkness just after midnight to investigate a haunting that routinely happened at two a.m. My family slept, the porch light was on, and I hit the road.

Most ghost stories are as sad as they are terrifying. This was Kentucky, after all, a hotbed of the paranormal, where there are more reported ghost sightings and supernatural events than you will see in New Orleans, another city world-famous for its hauntings. In Kentucky, we have an entire tourism industry based on the paranormal. A stellar example of working with what you've got to hand. Our ghosts are locally sourced.

Tonight we are dealing with something extreme.

The sighting I am on my way to observe, to understand, and to resolve, is disturbing. The kind of haunting that comes from someone difficult in life . . . and malevolently dangerous in death.

He does not rest easy, this one.

I am a neurosurgeon but my consultations with patients that come to me through my NGO, the Enlightenment Project, are dark and deadly work. Lola Strickler came to me because I have a wealth of experience with hard and terrifying things, be it brain tumors, cognitive decline, psychosis . . . or the dark abyss of something *other.* The one thing my Enlightenment Project patients share is the desperation of people with their back to the wall. They have issues that don't fit into a well-defined category. Their symptoms feel mysterious. They struggle to understand. They lay awake at night, worrying.

Sometimes the source of trouble is physical; sometimes it is the fallout of trauma, remembered or not. Sometimes it is the hard bloom of psychosis, which so often, as we are beginning to understand, begins in the gut. Paying attention to the neurons that run from the gut to the brain can be a path to healing.

The essential question for these patients is this: does the problem come from within—where standard medical treatments are their best bet—or does it come from without?

I am at the top of my game. Today I did a deep brain stimulation for a Parkinson's patient, followed up by an acoustic neuroma surgery for a thirty-year-old woman, a seven hour surgery, tricky, but I am fairly sure I got all of the malignancy. A tumor like that has a dark presence I recognize intuitively. My Parkinson's patient was home for dinner; my tumor patient will be able to leave the hospital in three days. I am quietly hopeful for both.

I wish I felt hopeful for Lola Strickler.

I was running late. My team was there ahead of me.

My partner in the NGO, an exorcist priest in high demand, was Perry Cavanaugh, formerly of the Episcopalian church. It had been a wrenching decision for him to leave what had been a lifetime calling. But he had long been fed up with the way misogyny and prejudice so often collided with the best interests of the people he wanted to help.

He'd been *my* exorcist when I was an eleven-year-old boy, bewildered and trapped and in the grip of a dark entity that almost took me down.

This is why I do what I do. I'm a neurosurgeon and I'm a healer and my perspective as a man who survived possession as a child means that I do not have the luxury of disbelief.

My phone chimed. A text from team member two, Chloe Donatello, married to Perry, estranged from him for years over their opposite views on religion vs. spiritual presence. They'd sorted it out when Perry left the church and now it was *game on* with the marriage.

Chloe was a brilliant quantum biologist who worked for the Enlightenment Project gratis, using our cases as insight into her commercial and academic research, always strictly confidential. One of her many formidable skills was the ability to track the trail and physical presence of supernatural entities. Mysterious dark matter presence could leave a biological marker. We were able to chart where it was, where it went, and if it was a specific entity or more than one—physical evidence, not conjecture. If there really was a ghost haunting Lola Strickler, Chloe would be able to find the trail and chart the path.

Sometimes knowing where a dark presence has been is terrifying. Knowing it has been there, watching, when you felt safe and unaware.

Chloe would do that tonight.

I glanced down at her text. Re: Pictures of entity forwarded to your phone from client Lola Strickler—authenticity confirmed. We're here. You're not.

But I was close. Lola lived downtown, three miles from my house, give or take.

Just before I turned off Fontaine Road onto East High Street, I caught a glimpse of headlights just in time to hit the brakes as a vintage gold Cadillac ran the light. Idiot driver. Cool car.

It was a half-moon night. Streetlights and stars. Fifteen minutes past midnight.

TWO

Lola Strickler, her cat, Virginia Kitty, and her husband, Jesse James Lynch, lived downtown in Hampton Court, off Third Street between Jefferson and Broadway. Tucked behind a beautiful stone arch, on a narrow lane where the houses and condominiums were built around 1907. Lola and Jesse lived in a red-brick four-story sprawling building, where attorney Charles H. Stoll developed the condominiums after tearing down an orphan asylum.

Some things never change.

Tucked into a quiet cul-de-sac off West Third Street, the condos were known for natural lighting, beautiful fireplaces, high ceilings, pocket doors, hardwood floors, and private oversized porch balconies.

I drove around the horseshoe lane that dead-ends into a pedestrian passage to the next street over, closed off with a gate. I parked across the street and sat for a moment, getting a feel for the place.

When Lola Strickler had called for an appointment, I was struck by what she had written on the intake form I require.

"I need someone to listen to me; I need someone to help. I'm three months pregnant and I'm being haunted, *harassed*, by a ghost. He comes in the darkness of early morning, just after two a.m. It was maybe once every ten days or so when it started up, and always at the same time, the same place. He stands on the sidewalk by the side of our condo building, while I'm outside on our second-floor balcony patio, where I go early in the morning to do my think work. I'm a musician, it's my creative time, more often than not I'm composing. No one else is up or awake then. I'm always out there alone. Also—he's coming more often now."

I'd met with Lola Strickler right away, in the Enlightenment Project clinic on Manchester Street, located in the Distillery

District in Lexington, Kentucky. She was about five-seven, slim, with long bony fingers. A charismatic presence, a certain gravitas. Her silky black skirt flowed softly past her knees, black tights, peacock-blue ankle boots with black buckles. She wore a man's blazer, reddish brown and patterned with tiny gold circles sewn with shiny thread. She'd folded the sleeves back behind her wrists. Her hair was dark, a layered blunt cut of reddish-brown mahogany swinging softly just past her collarbone, flipping up on the ends, wavy. I caught the glint of a gold chain around her neck, so narrow and fine you barely knew it was there. She wore a wide gold wedding band on her left hand.

I asked her why she thought she was being targeted. She looked away and shrugged. I asked if she had a history of any kind of supernatural event, any interest in ghosts or hauntings.

"No. Never. The closest I've come to the supernatural was reading Nancy Drew and *The Ghost of Blackwood Hall* when I was ten."

"Nothing else?"

She'd tilted her head to one side. "*The Ghost of Grey Fox Inn. The Ghost of the Lantern Lady.* I read all of the Nancy Drew books, and they're still on my bookshelf. There are a lot of ghost stories. They were thrilling when I was ten. They're comfort fiction now. Also *The Ghost and Mrs. Muir* by R.A. Dick. But whatever is haunting me . . . it's not a sexy sea captain . . . it's . . . nothing like that. This is evil. This is something that . . . It's coming after me. I feel like a target."

I'd nodded. Made a few notes. "And you say he always comes at the same time?"

"It's been the same time every night for the last two weeks. Two a.m."

"So now it's *every* night?"

She nodded.

"So it's escalating."

That worried me. It worried her too.

Lola was an internationally renowned sax player. Alto saxophone. At two a.m. every morning she woke up, full of mysterious creative energy—it was part of her process, a spiritual and inspired time to be still with her music, to compose, to plan the musical line-up for her ongoing performance schedule. She would sit out on the balcony, on the porch swing, curled up in a blanket, drinking a cup of coffee, cream and sugar. Often enough she would compose—she would have paper in hand and the music would come to her like a meditation and she'd work intensely until almost four a.m. then go back to bed. Lola taught music at Eastern Kentucky University, right down the road in Richmond, Kentucky, known for a faculty of performing musicians. Her specialty: jazz. She'd been a saxophone prodigy since the age of eight. She was much in demand at local venues, performed and taught nationally and internationally.

At first the man, the ghost, the apparition—the *whatever*—when he only came once in a while, she'd never been able to see him clearly. He was skittish, he didn't stay long, his features seemed blurred, hard to make out in the dark. She thought he was a new neighbor, being annoying and intrusive, staring up at her from the street. Those first times, he barely stayed long enough for her to see him clearly. And then he started getting closer, bolder. Twice now she'd leaned over the balcony, glaring at him. Took his picture on her phone. Told him to leave. Told him she was calling the police.

She sometimes had trouble with men, she told me, which was no surprise. All women have trouble with certain kinds of men. She had dismissed him as a neighborhood perv, and she'd reported him to the police twice. They had come out to her house the second time, when Jesse wasn't home. She'd given them the same pictures she'd given me.

Once she had called the police while he was looking at her, talking loud enough for him to hear her, showing him the phone, telling him to leave. He didn't seem to clock what she was saying. Like they were in two different worlds. He just stood on the sidewalk, staring up at her, smoking a cheap white-tipped cigar. Oh, and that was a thing. He was always smoking those cigars. Were there really ghosts who smoked? Did that make any sense? And it was real, she could smell the cigar smoke, wasn't that weird?

It wasn't weird though. It was a normal manifestation. As much as a manifestation can be considered normal.

I'd asked her to text me the pictures she had of him on her phone. Half expecting them to be hazy, hard to make out, murky. As they so often are. But they had come through in detail.

A tall man, six-four or six-six, slim, rangy. He looked to be in his early sixties, pure white hair razored short on the sides, thick and wavy on top. Face a map of age lines, lips tight and angry. He was looking up at Lola with the furious malevolence I had seen not in ghosts but in dark entity possessions. The really bad ones are steeped in rage. He always wore a wrinkled white shirt, buttoned tight to the neck, collar curling. Khakis pulled high up on his waist, worn silver-tipped leather belt.

If he was coming after Lola, she was in trouble.

"You look worried," she said.

"I'm taking this seriously, Lola. I'm glad you are too."

"So here's a thing I don't understand. Now, just this past week . . . he's started singing. 'Moon River'."

He would stare at her while he sang it, with a bewildering intensity, as if the song should mean something to her. And he was getting closer, bolder, standing on the sidewalk almost under the balcony, staring up at her.

"What does your husband think? He's seen this?"

She would not meet my eyes. "This is not about my husband."

"Are you telling me he hasn't seen the ghost or that he doesn't know about any of this?"

"Both. He hasn't seen the ghost, and I haven't told him anything about this."

Hell of a red flag. "Are you worried he won't believe you? I'm sorry, but I have to ask. If you haven't told him about this, even when you thought the guy was a pervy neighbor, that makes me wonder why. It makes me think you don't trust him, that maybe he's a problem."

"That's not it."

"Are you safe with your husband, Lola?"

Her cheeks flared red. "I adore my husband. He is the best man I have ever known. This is not what you think."

"I'm not sure what I think."

"My husband is having serious health issues right now. I had a miscarriage eight months ago and we were both just . . . devastated. We're both scared it will happen again."

I gentled my voice. "I understand." And I did. Moira and I had known that grief before we adopted our sons.

"He's having a really rough time, physically. He's having some kind of attacks, and I'm worried about his heart, but he thinks it's neurological. He's afraid he has a brain tumor. He's gone to see a slew of doctors and they just keep bumping him to other doctors and running tests, and it's a nightmare and—"

"Tell him to come and see me," I said. "I'll get him in right away."

"Will you?"

"Yes. But I do need to know if *you're* safe."

She nodded. "I'm safe with Jesse. I'm not safe with this . . . thing."

"Understood." I studied her, trying to read her. I was suspicious of her husband. Wondering if her fear of him was manifesting into seeing a ghost. According to Chloe, the pictures she'd taken had been the real deal. Still. Her husband was the question here.

"When did Jesse's symptoms start?" I asked her.

"Right about the time I got pregnant. So I think it's stress over that. And . . ." She stopped. "Oh. Same time I started seeing the ghost."

"Something to factor in." The onset of his symptoms dovetailing with Lola seeing the entity made me uneasy. The world is ever suspicious of husbands, and I was no different. But it might well mean he was as affected by this presence as she was. Aware of it on an intuitive, psychological level. Dark entities have a strong effect on the people unlucky enough to be around them. Their malevolent presence can cause depression, suicide, and illness, leaving the people affected bewildered and at escalating risk. Time is on their side, not yours, and they are insidious. Jesse and Lola being secretive, and not confiding in each other, did not mean they weren't both affected. But it added another layer of worry for Lola's safety. I have learned the hard way to listen, to pay close attention to the fears and intuition of my patients. They may not know how they know things, but they are so often right.

Lola was at considerable risk—be it from a dark entity, a husband in distress, a past trauma, or all of the above. And not just Lola. It looked like Jesse was in trouble too. I was worried about their baby. I'd have to sort it.

Whoever or whatever was putting Lola Strickler at risk, she was three months pregnant, vulnerable, and caught between a mysterious malevolent ghost and an unraveling husband. The stakes could not be higher.

Tonight, at two a.m., my team and I would be ready to observe, to record, and to keep Lola safe.

Tonight, we'd be waiting for this malevolent presence who was stalking her. I wondered if he would come tonight. I wondered if he would sing.

THREE

I got out of the car, but I didn't go in. I walked around to the side of the condo. Stood still. If something was there or had been there, I might feel it. My history of possession meant I was acutely attuned to dark presence. A skill set I could do without. Walking around the brick building, I was immediately uneasy. In a way that was familiar. I was wide awake now, alert, looking up at the balcony, glowing with the light from inside the condo.

I wanted to see what the entity was looking at.

I imagined Lola looking down. Afraid. How it would feed on that, would crave her attention, smug and powerful when she acknowledged it, talked to it. Let it into her life. The more they interacted, the stronger the pathway between them.

I wondered if anyone else saw him. Any of the neighbors. Lola had not wanted me to ask, and I understood that. These kinds of sightings are held close and secret. It is never safe to share these things with the world.

I glanced down at the grass, the edge of the sidewalk. White-tipped cigar butts, three of them, wet with the rain we'd had last night. I put on a glove, secured them into a baggie. It is rare for a ghost to leave physical evidence. We would run DNA testing. There are no rules to this kind of thing because we know so little about the world of dark matter and spiritual presence. But the more physical evidence the better.

Likely there would be no physical traces on the cigar. But it was possible. If it had left biological markers of any kind, Chloe would find them.

I stood for a moment. Still. Looked over my shoulder suddenly, feeling like I was being watched by something curious and unfriendly. It seemed to come from a cluster of trees. I headed that way, then stopped. Nothing. But something had been there, and I had the uneasy feeling I had been observed. Noticed. Clocked.

I headed around the sidewalk to the entrance, passing through the wooden double doors into a marble-floored lobby, heading up the wide staircase to the second floor. It was the kind of place where people had Wolf gas stoves and clawfoot tubs.

Lola said she had great neighbors, the kind of neighbors who welcomed the music when she practiced late afternoons or early evenings.

Likely while they were cooking gluten-free sweet potato gnocchi. I won't lie to you: I like gluten-free sweet potato gnocchi myself.

Lola came to the door like she'd been standing there waiting for my knock, greeting me with a tense smile, welcoming me in. It was a pretty place, old radiators painted white, walls slate grey with white trim, black and white checkerboard tiles in the kitchen and laundry room. It was wide open and big. High ceilings, a fireplace in the living room, pocket doors dividing off the bedrooms, and a clubby Restoration Hardware leather couch that was oversized and took up a lot of the room. A black and orange cat was curled up on the coffee table, stretched out over some sheet music with crossed-out notations.

Virginia Kitty gave me the once-over, then tucked herself up more comfortably and I could hear her purr from across the room. I would keep an eye on her, though she seemed fairly tame. As tame as cats go. It was rare for me to meet a cat that did not try to make me bleed as a way of saying *hello, you are not welcome here*. Even our own family cat had only just resigned himself to tolerating me, instead of slashing my ankles as a way of saying hello.

Lola looked comfy in black calf-length yoga tights, a tucked-in black tee, and an oversized white button-up shirt hanging loose, with the sleeves rolled up. Thick socks and classic high-topped white Reeboks in a style that was so old it had become retro and back in demand. I knew this because Moira wore them too.

She had told me she was three months pregnant, and I would never suspect a woman of miscalculating, but she was showing a small and healthy round belly already.

Perry was sitting on the couch drinking coffee, looking comfortable in dad jeans and a thin worn-out sweater. There were cake crumbs on his lap, and on the coffee table in front of him were unwrapped Hostess CupCakes, chocolate and orange, on a big plate, with a stack of napkins.

Lola picked up the plate and offered it to me. "The orange ones are so good," she said. "But take a chocolate one too. I know that serving Hostess CupCakes means I will never have membership in the cool-kids club, but they are the only thing I can keep down—that and Ritz crackers." She gave me a smirk. "So hard to live on cupcakes, but I struggle on."

That was when she charmed me.

I took one of each as directed and said yes to coffee. She brought me a mug out of the kitchen that had paw prints on it and said *MAMA BEAR* on the side.

"Is Papa Bear here?" I asked. Still standing.

Lola looked crushed. "No. Jesse's working late. I scheduled it that way on purpose."

I set the cupcakes on a napkin, held my coffee, and waited. She sat at the other end of the couch.

"It's past time to tell him, Lola. You've been afraid for weeks."

She shrugged. "Better for him not to know."

"He'll know something. He'll know you're acting different. He'll worry. It's going to be hard for me to go much further without him knowing. I want you to commit to telling him after I leave tonight."

She looked away.

"For your good and his. He's made an appointment to see me this week. I'm not comfortable—I can't really be a good doctor to him if I can't talk about what is going on in your house. Even if he doesn't know it's there, he'll feel it."

She froze. "Could that be . . . could that be what's causing his physical symptoms?"

"I won't know until I run some tests, but I have to be able to tell him the truth. And we need to get his take on things."

"He doesn't have a take or he'd have told me."

I waited. But this was the south, and everybody kept everything secret. Truth telling in this part of the country was always a hard sell.

"I'll think about it," she said.

"If you want to do what's best for Jesse, you'll tell him."

"But for now—"

"For now, Lola, let's see if your ghost shows up."

"He'll show up. He's here like clockwork now. Every night at two a.m."

FOUR

Lola had deep purple circles under her eyes, from worry and lack of sleep. The energized woman who kept giving me Hostess CupCakes had faded.

"He didn't come," she said softly. "I thought he would come."

The look that she gave me was full of anguish. Like a woman who did not think she would be believed, like a woman who was afraid she was going to have to deal with things alone.

I was standing in front of the fireplace. "That's not unusual. They don't come on demand. But I *do* think he was around. I think he was close. I did a walk around the condo before I came to your door. There was something out there."

I waited for her to ask me how I knew that but she didn't.

She chewed a swatch of hair. "He's been here every night at the exact same time for the last two weeks."

"He's fucking with you, hon," Chloe said over her shoulder. "Like all men, living or dead. But listen, this has been a good first session, and progress has been made."

As always, Chloe was deeply absorbed in her work, her thoughts, her calculations, and also able to catch every nuanced emotion of everyone in the room. She was never distracted; she was always absorbed.

"*First* session? I thought maybe you could do some kind of exorcism thing and make him go away. Or do you not do that with ghosts?"

Chloe gave me a look, but it was Perry who sat beside Lola. For a spiritual warrior he had a gentle side.

"Tonight is about getting a take on exactly what we're dealing with, and then we'll make a plan, and you'll be a part of that. Which, *yes*, is going to include an exorcism if we can pin him down, even just confirm his presence. That may be all we need."

Perry was dreaming, but he didn't know what I did. One exorcism wasn't going to cut it with this guy. This was no average exorcism of a haunted house, to make the sigh of ingrained presence shimmer and fade. This was something else entirely. I gave him a look and his smile faded.

Lola did not notice. She was watching Chloe, who was packing away her equipment. We were all watching Chloe, her dark blonde bed-head hair, the shiny knee-high black boots, well-worn and comfy, her air of being aware of things the rest of us did not even know existed. The world was bigger and more interesting to Chloe, and the rest of us were in a constant state of wondering what she would say next.

"We've made progress," Perry said. "We've switched out the porch light for a camera on the balcony, which will have a feed into your phone and also to mine, if you're OK with that."

She nodded. "Yes, I'm OK with that. So you'll catch him here another time?"

"I've already caught him here tonight," Chloe said with a smug smile. "We've got plenty of physical evidence, believe me; your guy here has been a busy boy. Let me show you."

"*Wait*," I said. "Lola. We'll show you everything if you want to know everything. But you can also say no thanks and leave it to us."

"Of course I want to know. Wouldn't you?"

"I would. Chloe?"

"OK, so this works a lot like luminol and bloodstains, like you've seen on cop shows on TV. Except it's completely different technology because this is microbial imaging tech, thank you, Zurich. What it does is lock on to the trail of destruction left by dark matter. And when we clock the specific high axion concentration the entity leaves behind, it's like their very own DNA. Basically, we're following a trail of destruction on the micro level."

Lola nodded, folding her arms tightly across her chest. "I don't really get the science."

"None of us do," Perry said. "Except my wife."

Chloe blew him a kiss, then looked over at Lola. "Can I set my laptop up on your coffee table there?"

"Yes. Of course."

"Gather round, my chickens." Chloe was completely absorbed with that high she gets from tracking dark things. "OK, so I'm using the dollhouse simulation. Which is just what it sounds like. This is your apartment, with one wall gone, and we can see inside. Everywhere you see red footprints—

"He leaves footprints?"

"No, not really, that's just the simulation. But when you see those footprints, that's where we've found the bio marker traces he's left. So you can think of it as footprints, bec-ause that's where he's been. Wreaking havoc like they always do."

"But you said . . . are you saying you've found him *inside* the apartment?"

"You found him inside?" I asked. "How recent?" I appreciated the song and dance and Lola needed to see the song and dance, but there were things I needed to know and I was running out of patience.

"Dark red, within the last twenty-four hours. Pinkish and barely there, three days ago. I did the balcony, and every room in the apartment."

I kept my facial expression casual, thinking *shit shit shit*. "Lola, you don't have to watch this tonight while you're alone. We can wait—"

"Better to know," she said in a hard voice.

Perry nodded. "That's how I'd see it."

"Ready?" Chloe asked.

Lola nodded. A line of tears rolling slowly down her cheeks.

"OK then. You're brave, and that's good. This thing has invaded your space and we're going to kick it the fuck back out."

I was relieved to see Lola smile.

"Just so you know. We're good at this. We've seen a lot of . . . a lot of shit. We always win."

Which wasn't true, but I wasn't going to interrupt the pep talk. And Chloe was on a roll.

"You're not going to face this alone," she said. "You've got us. And we kick ass. But I'm thinking you kick ass pretty good too."

Lola was trembling but she looked better.

"OK then. I'm going to start outside on the balcony and we can follow from there."

The footprints on the balcony were flaming deep red. And there were none of the spotty, here-again-there-again mild traces that I was used to seeing. Red on the bottom rail of the balcony, then the top, like he was physically climbing over. He'd walked in a circle then another circle, then sat in the middle of the porch swing.

Lola sat forward. "He was *on* the balcony."

"Likely for the first time tonight," Chloe said. "This is recent, and I'm not seeing any other destruction trails. The old ones show up differently. More like scars than wounds."

But I was looking at the glass door leading from the balcony into the apartment. Huge round red flaring at about six feet off the ground. Like he had his face smashed against the glass, looking in at us the whole evening. Like he was trying to get in right through that glass.

"He sat in my swing." Lola's voice had gone from horror to rage. "*Mother. Fucker.* I would kill him if he wasn't already dead."

Chloe laughed and I could not resist a smile.

"There you go," Perry said.

Chloe gave us a minute, letting Lola enjoy being mad instead of afraid. I liked how good she was with Lola. I like how she empowered Lola. But if she thought Lola needed a break and a breather, it meant worse was to come.

"Nothing in the kitchen," Chloe said. And I knew she was saving the worst for last. "Nothing in the little pantry."

"Show me the nursery," Lola said. "We've already started setting it up."

Chloe hesitated. "OK, here we go."

A rocking chair. A little dresser, painted yellow and white. Unpacked boxes and bags of baby clothes.

Pink on the back of the rocking chair, like he'd pushed the chair and let it rock. A smear like a handprint on one of the boxes.

"This is stuff we bought months ago, before my miscarriage."

"He wasn't there then," Chloe said. "I'd say four or five days ago on this."

Lola nodded. "Anything in the bathroom?"

"Nothing," Chloe said. "Thank God."

Lola let out a breath. "That's good anyway. Bedroom."

"Bedroom," Chloe said. "This one disturbs me, Lola."

It wasn't good. Nothing on the bed. But on a chair, across from the bed on the left side near the closet door, there were layers. Faded pink, pinkish white that was more of a shimmer than a color, strong pink, red. And a smear of red across the pillow on the left side of the bed.

Lola did not look away from the screen. "Interpret this for me, Chloe."

"Which side of the bed do you sleep on?" Chloe asked.

"Left side."

Chloe nodded. Took a breath. "OK, look, this is exactly what we need to know. He's been sitting across from the side of the bed where you sleep, and my take is he's been watching you for a while now, and quite regularly."

"How long a while?"

"How many weeks pregnant are you?"

"Twelve or thirteen."

"Well, I'll be the one who's going to say it. This is not good news. He's been watching you, I'd say, sometime between the first and second week you conceived. How long have you been seeing him outside?"

"I was figuring that out this afternoon. The first time I saw him I'd have been about one and a half weeks along."

"Interesting timing," Chloe said.

Lola put a fist to her mouth. "My God. Jesse knew all along."

"Meaning what?" I asked her.

"Just . . . what you said earlier. That on some level he's aware. He senses something off, something scary. Because my husband has been exhausted since before we even knew I was pregnant. He doesn't sleep. He sits up in bed, pretends to read motorcycle maintenance manuals, and watches *me* sleep. Every single night since I got pregnant. I thought it was just anxiety, because of the miscarriage. But maybe on some level he knows something is there. And his protective instincts kick in. And now this is beginning to make sense."

"How so?" I asked her.

She turned to look at me. "I know who it is."

FIVE

Lola went to a bookcase next to the television and started moving books off the shelves. I went to help. Nancy Drew. Two shelves packed tight, different editions through the years. Worn blue clothbound books, yellow ones with the title in a square of blue. She handed me one last stack, then reached back and pulled out an old eighties photo album, thick, brown cross-hatched binding, and laid it out on the coffee table.

"Do you have the pictures I sent? Can you pull them up on your laptop, Chloe?" Lola asked.

"Of course."

One click and there they were. Two shots of the man stalking her; exactly the ones I had on my phone.

"I just kept thinking this guy looked familiar, or I'd seen him before. And more than once. Like maybe I knew him or something, which didn't seem right, but still. I didn't think he was just some rando I'd seen in the neighborhood. But I could not get it out of my head that I'd seen him before. And then one day I was hanging out in the bathroom talking to Jesse—I like to watch him shave, I don't know why, I just do."

I don't know why women like to watch men shave, but Moira did the same.

Lola was frowning. "And you know, the way he had his head tilted, standing to one side, it struck me. This ghost . . . I realized he looked a little like my Jesse, and then it began to dawn on me. It didn't seem possible, but just in case . . . I dug up Jesse's old photo album from back when people had photo albums, and there he was. Jesse's dad. Erebus Lynch."

"Jesse's *father*?" I said.

She nodded. "And don't you see, that's the whole reason I didn't tell Jesse or want him to know anything about any of this. Because the guy I'm seeing—he's been dead since Jesse was fourteen years old."

She opened the album at a page marked with a sticky note. Perry, Chloe, and I all leaned in to see a photo of Erebus Lynch as a young father with a toddler Jesse riding on his shoulders.

It was the same man, unmistakable, just the young father version. Tall, rangy, slim, khaki pants buckled high up on his waist, cotton broadcloth shirt, white, buttoned tightly to the neck, but with a sleeveless knit sweater vest in a gray herringbone pattern. Thick dark blonde bowl-cut hair, an oddly defiant look for a man giving his little son a piggyback ride. In the second picture he was standing beside a teenage Jesse. Anger masked by a smile. A possessive arm around his son's shoulder. A son who was leaning away.

"I think he's dangerous," she said softly, as if afraid I would not believe her.

"I think so too. It's rare, you know, for a ghost, a manifestation, to be dangerous. Unless this is more than a haunting. Unless this is something else."

"What kind of else?"

"What kind of spiritual beliefs did Jesse's father have?" Perry asked.

"I don't know. I don't think he was religious, but I only know him from the way he treated Jesse and my mother-in-law and I have always hated him for that. Sorry. I'm passionate about this kind of thing." She turned back to me. "What kind of 'else'? Tell me what you mean."

"A dark entity. Not human. Malevolent." I had always wondered what happened to people who had died when they were possessed. When they became completely lost to the darkness.

Lola flinched. "*Malevolent*."

"And the first time you saw him you were pregnant with this child? You didn't see him for the pregnancy you lost eight months ago?"

She shook her head. "No."

"And Jesse was OK back then? You were OK back then?"

She nodded. "We were fine. We were . . . we were so happy. About the baby. Jesse took time off after the loss, and so did

I, just to face it, not shove it away. Nobody gives you time to grieve this kind of thing and we decided, fuck the world, we would. Our baby was loved. We couldn't go on like business as usual. We just jumped in the car and drove, a three-week road trip, and it . . . it was exactly what we needed. Nothing mattered but being together with the only other person who gets it, who's in it with you, we felt like we were back to back, together against the world."

"So this new pregnancy . . . this is the only major change in your life?"

"Yes."

I didn't like the sound of that. And by the expressions on Perry and Chloe's faces, they weren't keen on it either.

"Do you think this has something to do with my baby? This baby in particular? Does that sound crazy?"

But it didn't sound crazy. I wish that it had.

"I have a question for you, Lola, and I want you to think before you answer. When you see a manifestation like this, it's usual to feel a strong emotion. I'm not talking about the fear that we all have when we see something supernatural, something we don't expect. I'm talking about the emotional impact of the ghost—are they so sad they make you sad? You will sense their emotion and you will feel it too. What do you get from Erebus Lynch?"

"Oh, I know damn well what that emotion is. I don't have to think. Hatred. Jealousy. Rage. *At me*, and now at my baby. He doesn't just want me dead; he wants to kill my baby. *This* baby. I don't know how but I know he does."

"Was he like that when Jesse was growing up? Dangerous like that?" Chloe asked.

"I don't think so. I think he was just your everyday entitled asshole."

"So my question is—what was he like then compared to what he is like now?" I asked.

"Like maybe he's worse now for some reason?"

"Yes, exactly that. He was maybe kind of a jerk when Jesse was a kid, but now it's on a whole other level. Something dangerous. Something dark."

I hesitated. "What if all of the anger Jesse's father had attracted something. Something dark. Something that fed on it, and amplified it, until the dark thing took over and became the Erebus Lynch you are seeing now."

She thought about that. "And that's what brought him back? I . . . it's hard for me to know. I think only Jesse or his mom could answer that. But maybe that's a good thing. Maybe that means you can zap it with an exorcism and make it go away."

It's never a good thing. But I didn't tell her that.

"Can you tell us about Jesse's relationship with his father?" Perry asked.

"Yeah. Jesse has talked about it a lot ever since we decided to have babies. He is so afraid he'll be like his dad. So he's been doing some writing about it, seeing a therapist. He wants to be a good father like Ray and be nothing like his dad."

"And who is Ray?"

"His stepfather. He and his mom moved in with Ray as soon as Jesse's father died. So fast really that it was obvious they'd had a thing for a long time before his father died. She was in love with Ray before she met Jesse's dad. I'm not sure what happened. And Jesse had a very fraught relationship with his dad. You know, it was back in the bad old days when Jesse's mom got pregnant and they *had* to get married." Her face went hard. "Erebus Lynch was a terrible father, entitled, self-centered, codependent, pushing Jesse to have a certain kind of life. He wanted Jesse for himself. To have no one else. And he wanted Jesse to be a basketball player because he played basketball and had a basketball scholarship which he gave up when Jesse was born. He still went to college, got a business degree, and spent his life just whining over it, so sure he'd have been a hotshot athlete, and it was always all about him. But Jesse's mother . . . I mean she had to drop out of college, and she never said a word about that. She was pregnant, and she worked so Jesse's dad could finish school and nobody ever thought that was unfair, which it so is. But she wasn't this weak little pushover. She wouldn't have married Jesse's dad if she hadn't wanted to. She kept him in check. Like . . . Jesse hated basketball, but his dad made him practice two hours every day after school, until one day Jesse's mom just made it stop."

"How?" Chloe asked.

Lola gave us a sideways smile. "You wouldn't have to ask me that if you'd ever met Jesse's mother. She's . . . she's confident, tough, and gets what she wants. Catnip to men. Why she stayed with Erebus so long, I do not know. Jesse thinks she loved him but I find that hard to believe. I gave up trying to understand her. I avoid her. But she and Jesse are really close and she's a good mom. She'll be a good grandmother, I think, so long as she understands she's not in charge.

"But his dad . . . Jesse hated him. He always said he never, ever once loved his father. Which, when you think about it, is kind of strange. My mother-in-law won't talk about him to me. She just gets this stricken look when his name comes up and changes the subject. A lot of secrets there, I think."

"Any idea why he's coming to you? And not Jesse?" I asked.

"No idea. But he's *targeting* me. He's haunting me. Stalking me."

Whatever was haunting her was malevolent, and not exactly human now. The ghost of Erebus Lynch, or what was left of him, was completely lost to the darkness.

The only question in my mind was why *this* baby? Why not her previous pregnancy?

"Do you think he wants to kill my baby?" she asked again.

"I don't know."

"You *do* know."

"I think you're right. He's after you. He's after your baby. And I'm not going to let that happen. *We're* not going to let that happen."

She put a hand over her face. "Please. *Make him stop*."

"Yes," I said. "I will make him stop."

SIX

I lifted a hand to wave to Chloe and Perry as they passed me in their car.

Chloe rolled her window down. "Everything OK?"

"Not sure I'd say that, but I'm going to wait in my car until Jesse gets here. I don't want to leave her alone, not tonight when this thing is riled up."

"We can stay too," Perry offered.

"No, go home, but I wanted to give you this, Chloe." I handed her the bag of cigar tips. "I found those outside, before I came in, under the balcony where Lola said Lynch always stood and smoked when he watched them. Not sure what you'll find."

She took the bag and shrugged. "I have no idea what I'll find. Just not DNA."

"We don't need DNA. We know who he is."

"What we don't know is *what* he is," Perry said. "Erebus Lynch is long dead."

They waved and headed off. Exhausted, all of us were.

But I wasn't going to leave until Jesse got home.

I headed toward the trees where I'd felt the presence earlier. Nothing now but the wind and the smell of a jasmine bush that someone had planted on the side of the condo. It wouldn't survive the winter, but for now it was still thriving in early fall, still hot enough out for it to be lush and green and covered in white star-shaped flowers, and I stayed on the edge of the sidewalk under a black walnut tree, melting into the shadows. Hoping to see Jesse Lynch and not his father.

I heard the deep rumble otherwise known as "the sound of excellence"—the unmistakable engine of a Ducati motorcycle, something I had yearned for since I was a kid. Unaffordable when I was young, unaffordable when I was in med school.

Affordable now but I was a neurosurgeon and I had seen too many traumatic brain injuries to ride one now. Not with a wife and two young sons at home.

Jesse James Lynch parked the bike with silky ease and I saw Lola open the front door and run to him down the steps. He was slim like his father, but not so tall, tight jeans, boots, leather jacket. Dark hair. Eyes only for his wife, as he set his helmet down and lifted her up and held her close.

"You OK?" he said. "You didn't sound good on the phone. What's going on, baby girl?"

A deep voice, resonant, full of confidence, and he didn't look the least bit fragile to me. I got a good feeling about him. He would keep Lola safe.

I smiled as I watched them bound up the stairs to the condo hand in hand. I would sleep better now that I'd seen them together.

I headed to my car, tossed my briefcase of notes and my investigation kit into the back seat. Sighed. I was tired as fuck.

I started the engine. And I smelled him before I saw him. The reek of evil. The reek of the grave. And the smell of cigar smoke. I looked in my rearview mirror and saw him staring at me. The curl of cigar smoke rising in the air.

This kind of presence was familiar to me. It brought back the afternoon on High Bridge where I'd had one leg over the edge, mesmerized by the mysterious red-haired man who was not really a man, who had come with my own possession. He had been goading me on, and I would have jumped, desperate, just a kid, back to the wall of despair.

And then I had seen my father. Dead for months, but he was there. He was with me. My father. Standing on the other side of the bridge, smiling at me. And I knew I was safe in the world. I had pulled back from the edge of that bridge, and the hard-core grief of losing my dad at the age of eleven leveled out. Because I had thought he was gone and I was wrong. He had always been close and he would always be close. Still keeping me safe in the world.

This man who was not really a man watched with pure unfiltered rage, the cigar smoke growing thicker in the car. We looked at each other in the rearview mirror, me and Erebus Lynch. And I sensed it. The presence inside him. Unmistakable to a man like me who had known that presence myself.

Erebus Lynch was dead. Erebus Lynch was possessed. How much was him, and how much was other, I did not know.

I had always wondered what happened to anyone who died while possessed. I had thought—I had hoped—that the dark entity would leave once the victim died. Now I knew not. Now I knew the horror never ended. That it got worse and worse.

Would it be possible to set Lynch free, and end this once and for all?

Exorcisms were Perry's skill set. But Perry wasn't here, and words are powerful, full of vibration and harmonic resonance.

"I ask for your safety, Erebus Lynch," I said. "I ask that you be wrapped in the bright white light of protection, strength, honor and grace, reborn in a baptism from the darkness that has settled within you. I ask that you be freed from the wandering evil that has inhabited your soul."

And he began to sing. "Moon River". And the way he sang it, it felt like a warning, it felt like a threat, and I wondered what that song had meant in his life, and why the sound of it in his deep, resonant voice made the hair stir on the back of my neck. And I understood now why Lola had felt such a horror to hear him singing.

So I began to sing it back to him. To throw him off balance, to fuck with him, to see what he would do.

I felt it like a fog around me. The palpable rage he emanated. The car began to rock from side to side, so hard I thought it was going to flip, and I hung on to the steering wheel, hit my head on the window, hard.

Then the car settled and was still, and I turned to the back seat. No one there, not that I could see or feel.

I rolled all the windows down. Breathed for a while.

Tomorrow I'd ask Chloe to scan the car and track the trail of his presence. It was personal now, and I was going to be looking over my shoulder until I got this sorted. I headed home. Remembering my father with gratitude, and the quiet joy that grief eventually and miraculously becomes. What my life would have been without a man like my father, I do not know. How it was for Jesse to have a father like Erebus Lynch was hard to fathom, but I understood his fear. That he would somehow become the man his father was.

Erebus Lynch had me in his sights. And I had him in mine.

We were in for it now.

SEVEN

I arrived home in darkness, just before dawn. My headlights caught the shape of a woman sitting in one of the rocking chairs on our front porch with a dog at her feet. My dog, Tash, stretched out beside her. I caught enough detail to know this was not Moira. This was no one I knew.

I parked the car and got out quickly. I could see her under the porch light as I got closer.

Elderly, thin, thick grey hair in a braid pinned and circled around her head. She wore a loose dress, her skin sagging, and she tilted her head and looked up at me. Tash wagged her tail.

"Ma'am," I said. "Do I know you? Are you lost?"

"I am right where I want to be." Her voice was soft and steady, confident. But she seemed tired and frail, as if it took all of her energy just to sit in that chair.

I pulled up another rocking chair and sat close. In her nineties, I thought, and fragile. Tash sat up and laid her head in the woman's lap.

"Do you know where you are?" I asked her.

She gave me a serious look. "Do you?"

I took a breath, let it out slowly. I was tired. "Let me help you get home. Is there someone I can call?"

"I'm here to see you," she said.

I caught the scent of perfume. White Shoulders, the kind my great-grandmother used to wear.

"How can I help you, ma'am?" I would call emergency services. Someone must be looking for her.

She patted my hand. "No need for that. I'm here because I'm worried about my great-grandson, Liam. You'll be meeting him soon. It is a synchronicity for the two of you to intersect, and there is a lot of synchronicity in your life right now. Warring spiritual forces masquerading as coincidence."

'I think you're confused, ma'am."

"Did you see a gold Cadillac tonight?"

I stopped. Felt a chill. "Yes, I did."

"And now neither of us are confused. You're the one Liam must meet, and it can only be you, because you walked the path of darkness as a child."

She had to be referring to the possession.

"You know about that?"

She gave me a soft look. "It's a terrible thing, and you know it. You found a better way. You were lucky. You were strong. I hope that Liam will find a better way too, and you are the only one who will understand him. I'd like you to take a picture of the two of us sitting together on this porch, and when the times comes—and you'll know it, if and when it does—I want you to show it to him. I would ask that you tell Liam that I was grateful when he stopped his mother from cutting my hair short while I was ill. That I want for him to become again the hero who defended me when he was so young. Will you do that? Please know that I'll find a way to return the favor."

"How did my dog get out here?"

"She asked, and I answered."

Sweet Tash, who liked this woman, and made no move to leave her side. Like she was bewitched. And I had seen the gold Cadillac. I pulled out my phone. Took the picture.

She had a lovely smile. "Thank you, Noah Archer."

"Can I help you up out of the chair? Drive you home?"

She let me take her arm. She weighed so little, fingers soft and light on my shoulder as I helped her down the stairs.

"I'll walk now," she told me. "But remember this. In the spiritual warfare of synchronicity, which masquerades as omens, portents, and coincidence, you'll have to decide the meaning—the good of it, the bad of it. Your gut instinct will let you know if it's warning, reassurance, or the path. You'll have choices to make. Hard ones. You're a powerful man, Noah Archer. You can raise the dead."

Tash barked sharply and I glanced at her over my shoulder.

When I looked back, the pinkish-orange light of dawn was lifting the darkness, and the woman was walking slowly and steadily down the sidewalk. As the sky flooded with light, she shimmered and was gone.

EIGHT

A week after we had our first session with Lola, the motion-activated camera still hadn't picked anything up, according to Perry, who was keeping tabs. Which did not mean there wasn't anything there. Tech has limitations.

Lola was also checking in with Perry every day, and she had sounded almost cheerful when he had talked to her. But I was uneasy and so was Perry. We knew that whatever inhabited Erebus Lynch would see my impromptu exorcism as an attack. Things always got worse before they got better—in exorcism, as in everything else, every action has an equal and opposite reaction, and Erebus Lynch was more dangerous now than he was before. What he would do next, I did not know. Just that it would likely be violent, unexpected, and dark.

A few days ago, I'd had my first appointment with Jesse. Earlier this morning I had looked over his test results and come up with a snap diagnosis. Sometimes called "the terror of the father". The baby on the way, the presence of his father around him unaware, all of it triggering the fallout of his childhood under the pressure of an intense codependent relationship that went beyond love and hard into the territory of psychological abuse.

I am well aware that the term *codependency* can be aimed unkindly at relationships that are as loving as they are troubled. I am talking about something else—the traumatic whipsaw of an obsessed, powerful, and terrifying father. Demanding, insatiable, giving everything in extremes—except what a son really needs. An independent path of his own. This kind of father is charming and needy, charismatic and powerful. Overtaking the vulnerable boy who would resist, then run back in guilt to the beloved-hated father who played him so well and was impossible to please. And then the blowback as the adult man tried to process a childhood that had been a straitjacket of love, unhealthy sacrifice and ever-escalating expectations, building a fire of suppressed rage, shame, and guilt. Physically expressed memories coming through as physical issues with the body—some things *only* the body remembered, as the mind blocked it out. Generating anxiety in the extreme.

There are sons who give up. There are sons who fight back. Jesse James Lynch was a fighter but I could not forget another thing he'd said on the forms he'd filled out: "my father is in me, somehow." It rekindled my worry for Lola and their baby. My fear that Jesse might be as dangerous as his father. Jesse's own fears that he would become his father. Sons with fathers like this never seem to escape.

During our appointment, Jesse told me that in the last six weeks he'd experienced three panic attacks that caused him to pass out. So I had sent him for the usual barrage of tests that would be useful in ruling things out.

I had also encouraged him to talk, and I had gotten to know him a little. Jesse was so proud of Lola, in awe of her talent, telling me with a big smile how the two of them would play together sometimes, for local gigs. He was an absolute maniac on electric guitar. He owned his own garage—an intuitive master mechanic, who loved muscle cars, ancient Miatas, Ducati and vintage Indian motorcycles, though he would turn his hand to any engine, with the exception of a Tesla. He had a quirky passion for the Lawn-Boy lawnmowers from the eighties. He was something of a legend in town.

"My wife is pregnant," he'd said. "So I need to figure out what's going on with me and get it sorted." Definitely the proud dad-to-be. "We lost a baby a while back so we haven't told anybody Lola is pregnant again except for Mom and Ray and you. Ray is my stepfather. Great guy. Really just the best. Lola lost her mom when she was pretty young, but she says she knows she is close, watching over us. She talks about her mom a lot."

And it struck me. Lola felt her deceased mother would look after her. But Jesse was convinced his long-dead dad was a threat. So much so that he told me on the first visit that he would prefer a brain tumor to the reality of his father once again in his life.

As if a man can ever leave his father behind.

It was also very clear during the initial consultation that he and Lola still had not talked, which made me uneasy. I was frustrated with Lola for not confiding in him, but as baffling as it seemed to me, I well remembered that I had been just as secretive with Moira when my own past had come roaring back. She had never known that I had been possessed as a child, and I had been too afraid she would not want me if I told her. And when I had to tell her, she accepted my past but not the lie, and I came close to losing her over that. I do not know why it is so hard to tell the person you love most what you really need to say. I had just learned the hard way to do it.

It had been freeing, it had been hard, and now it was becoming second nature. And Moira and I were closer than ever.

Lola was going to have to talk to Jesse. That was the problem I would handle this afternoon when he came in for his test results.

NINE

They came in together, Jesse and Lola, holding hands and looking so connected and in love that I knew she had told him. My fears about Jesse being violent with Lola eased as soon as the two of them walked into my office. He was watching over her the same way I watched over Moira. They were young. Deeply in love. The energy between them was strong and confident. They were together, back-to-back against the world. They reminded me of Moira and me twenty years ago.

Jesse wore a black bomber jacket, worn jeans loose on his hips. He was slim, rangy, and tall like his dad, thick black hair short on the sides, wavy, combed back. He had the retro look of a fifties rock and roll star, and eyes that were electric and blue. He wore a wide gold wedding band matching the one Lola wore.

I gave them the results of the tests we'd run.

"You're as healthy as can be, Jesse." I could see that Lola thought this was good news. I could see that Jesse did not. "Because now I've done the tests—"

Jesse leaned forward. "You're sure it's not a brain tumor or cancer. Maybe fallout from an old head injury. I've had concussions; I've come off the bike more than once."

"Nothing I could find."

"OK." He gave me a grin. "How's life with the Daddy Car?"

"How's the Ducati?"

We'd talked bikes the last time he'd come in. My envy was palpable. He had a Ducati Diavel. The 2011. My dream ride.

Jesse shook his head. "I feel bad for you every time I start it up."

"I can't wait till you resign yourself to the Daddy Car."

"Man, that was cruel." Then his smile faded. "So nothing physical wrong with me. No meds, no surgery to make this go away."

"I can't help but feel bad for a guy whose last hope is a

brain tumor. We're going to sort your issues, Jesse, and it's going to be a whole lot easier to deal with panic attacks."

"And that's all they are?"

"*All* they are? They're formidable, but we'll sort it."

He glanced at Lola. "So, my wife and I have been talking."

I glanced up at Lola.

"Yeah," she said. "I told him. He was mad at first but then we sat down together and I found out he's been keeping a lot of stuff from me too. So secrets are out the window now. Everything is out there."

I wondered if that was true. It so rarely is.

"I thought you would think I'm a freak," he said to Lola.

I leaned back in my chair. "So what haven't you told me, Jesse? You say you're having issues regarding your father. God knows you are: he's haunting your wife. It could be the presence of your dad that's triggered the panic attacks. It could be a combination of that and other things. If I'm going to help you, you need to tell me what's really going on."

Jesse looked at Lola again and nodded. "Of course."

"The first time you panicked and passed out was two and a half months ago, right? And you don't know what triggered it?"

"Right."

"What was going on when it happened?"

Lola took his hand. "You were at the Opera House, weren't you?"

I looked up.

Jesse nodded again. "The Lexington Opera House. It's beautiful right?"

"Very," I said. Also very haunted. Lots of fizzy paranormal presence there, usually manifesting in electrical malfunction, flashing lights. There was no ghost legend attached, but the presence was most definitely there. And one thing led to another. It would be a ripe environment for Jesse's dad.

I did not bring that up.

"I was there to look it over. Finalize the arrangements with management for our own little opera. Lola and I . . ." He laughed and she sighed and gave him a tense little smile. "You know, I've been worried, what kind of dad I would be. When

Lola was pregnant before, and I was getting panicky . . . we decided to . . ." He faltered. Gave me a wide grin. "Exorcise my demons by writing our own opera. And we liked it so much we're in production as we speak. I'm a theater kid now, like Lola. A rock and roll opera. Every scene, with me in the spotlight, talking about one of my memories of my dad, and how I can be different. My fear of being just like him. To me he is the definition of a bad father. Followed up by a musical dance number. A tango. I learned to tango in college and I'm good."

"He's *really* good," Lola said.

Jesse grinned. "Lola's better. And there is a lot of music. Me on guitar, Lola on alto sax. We thought it would be therapeutic. And really . . . it has been. And it's good, Dr. Archer. The play."

"Tell him what it's called," Lola said with a quick glance at me.

Jesse grinned. "*Bad Dad Tango*."

I sighed. That would do it.

"And the two other times you passed out?"

"The other two were at the Manchester Music Hall, down in the Distillery District. We're doing our rehearsals there."

I nodded. "My NGO office is just about across the street."

"The warehouse?"

"Fourth floor. So . . . all three times happened at music venues. Never at home. Never at work. Never when you're just out and about."

He shook his head. "You think it's the play? The music?"

"Do you rehearse at home?"

"All the time," Lola said.

"So what's different?" Jesse asked.

I leaned back in my chair. "Do you know what you're afraid of? What you're thinking about before you pass out?"

"Well. Obviously my dad in the sense of the play, but usually I'm pretty absorbed in the rehearsal and it just seems to come right out of the blue."

"Things like this don't come out of the blue, Jesse. So if your dad was somewhere around, something on an intuitive level might sense his presence. And that could certainly cause a panic attack."

"That . . . that's interesting. It feels right. And also Lola—"

"Yeah, when it happens to Jesse, I feel tense and anxious and I don't even know why. I thought maybe it was an empathy thing."

"Except it's only when you're rehearsing the play. In a place where your dad could be watching you, but you don't know. We've tracked him inside your apartment, and it's likely he's there at the music hall too. I think he *is* there and both of you are aware of that on a subconscious level. Your brain is clocking his presence, because it's real, and it's a threat."

Lola grabbed Jesse's hand. "I think that's it. I think we both sense him there, because honestly, I get goosebumps and a chill down my back and—oh crap. He's watching us, Jesse. He's there." She looked at Jesse and then me. "And listen, guys, let's just say it. We know what he wants. At least I know what he wants. Me and my baby dead. So he can have Jesse all to himself."

"But why now?" I asked. "There has to be something else."

Jesse ran a hand through his hair and grimaced. "It doesn't matter what he wants. My whole life has been about what he wants. He's dead. I'm not letting that start back up again. I want him out. I want him gone, and I will kill him again if I have to. Can we please just make him go away?"

"Working on it." And I began to make some sense of it all. "So, Jesse. Your panic attacks make perfect sense, which means we can figure this out, there's a thread of logic. In the meantime—how are you sleeping? Your father is there in the bedroom sometimes and watching Lola, which means you stay awake to keep her safe. Are either of you getting any sleep?" Their exhaustion was palpable, which did not surprise me. Lots of worries. Lots of late nights. And if it went the usual way . . . a lot of *disturbed* nights.

"He doesn't sleep," Lola said. "He props up on a pillow and literally watches me sleep."

"Lola told me about the way you guys tracked my dad. That he's been watching her sleep at night. That makes sense to me, because that's when I have an overwhelming worry about her. I thought I was just being anxious, but—"

"But now we know you had a damn good reason. So you were being intuitive. On some level you knew. Trust your gut, Jesse," I said.

He nodded. "It's not just Lola who's seen my dad in the last few months. I was afraid you wouldn't believe me. I was afraid *she* wouldn't believe me. But that was before—"

"Before you found out I had been to your house trying to get the ghost of your father on film."

"Sounds weird to hear that out loud, but yeah, that's what I'm saying. I was afraid that if I told you I am being haunted by my father, you'd take it as some kind of metaphor or existential issue."

I nodded. It would be a hell of a lot easier if that was all that was going on. Existential looked pretty damn good right now.

"I need specifics please. I know what's going on with Lola. Give me the other half of the story and tell me what's going on with you."

He looked away. "You know, it's not just me and Lola who have seen things. Lola and I, we talked this over with Mom and Ray, and from the way they reacted they didn't seem surprised."

"His mother freaked out," Lola said.

"Yeah, she kind of did," Jesse said. "Which makes me think she's had trouble with Dad too, but she wouldn't say."

"I'd like to talk to her about that," I said. "If she's open to it."

Jesse nodded. "I'll let her know."

I felt that tingle at the small of my back that meant things were going to get intense. That was the thing about a possessed dark entity haunting. It wasn't just about you. It affected everyone you were close to. Everyone you loved.

"Start at the beginning, Jesse, and don't leave anything out."

"OK. So. At first it was like signs from the universe. I don't know if you believe in that, but things happened that . . . that meant him. Signs of him."

"I do believe in that. Read Carl Jung on Synchronicity. It will keep you up at night."

"I have, actually," Jesse said. "It scared me."

I nodded. I felt a stir of dread. People underestimate synchronicity, which can sometimes be a gift, sometimes a warning, and sometimes a threat. I had seen it be dangerous stuff. Meaningful coincidences, with no cause-and-effect chain of logic, were often a sign of paranormal events. And once things got rolling, you got a ghost in the back seat of your car and a mysterious great-grandmother on your front porch. She had called it a form of spiritual warfare. I was beginning to see her point. Warfare meant more than one side. That made me nervous.

"It started about two, two and a half months ago," Jesse went on. "I started seeing my father's car—a gold Cadillac. And not just any gold Cadillac. A 1968 Cadillac Eldorado Topaz Gold Firemist 472 V8. These days that is one rare car, and it was a standout back in the day. And it was *his* Caddy, like his right down to the whitewall tires and the greeny-gold diamond patterned cloth and vinyl interior." Jesse stopped. Looked at me. "What's wrong?"

"Not a thing." I gave him my most reassuring smile. I didn't tell him that I'd seen the car the night I went ghost hunting at his house. Or that I had seen it twice since. A classic gold Cadillac with Erebus Lynch behind the wheel. I had not had that calm sense of safety since that night at their condo. That you have when you are objective, helping, but it was not *you* at risk.

It happened this way, with the NGO cases. They got personal and I was drawn in, on a physical, mental and emotional level. That's what made this work dangerous. Things that *noticed* you, *wanted* you. There are no guardrails with a presence that has an altered structure of reality. At that point it is like being locked in. Synchronicity engaged.

"Go on. You're seeing your father's gold Caddy."

"*Unmistakable.* I've seen it in traffic, two or three cars behind. One night on my way home from the garage, it was doing a drive-by, slow, when I was locking up. After that I started seeing it in traffic, ahead of me, on the other side of the road, going the other way. Then . . . driving by on our street, slowing down when it went past our condo."

"So gradually getting closer. Does that sound accurate?"

"Yeah. I know what Lola means when she says she's being stalked. Except *we're* being stalked. And our baby. All three of us are in his sights."

He looked up at me. A question in his eyes.

"Exactly right. I think you are, all three of you. I don't think you're imagining anything and I think you're smart to be very aware of the danger."

I could see he was shaken. It is one thing to suspect and another entirely to know. But he and Lola needed to know.

"I've seen the Caddy cruise around that loop of our street. More than once. Sometimes I see it parked across the street, or in front of our building. Usually at night. When it's dark. By morning it's gone."

"So all the behaviors are escalating."

"Is it always like that?"

"It is when it's . . . trouble. The more you see it, the more you interact, the stronger the pathway between you. And hey—" I held up a hand. "You haven't done anything wrong. This is the dynamic and it's disturbing, but ignoring it would make it worse. It's a tightrope. Don't feed it, but you have to be aware, and you have to be smart. What this means, on a practical basis, is that we deal with it fast and hard. The longer we give it, the more entrenched it gets."

"Yeah. Lola and I, we're up for that. And funny you should say escalating. We had an incident. This morning. I didn't just see the car, Dr. Archer. I saw *him*. First I noticed the car behind me, on Clays Mill Road, when I was heading for Good Foods Co-op on Southland Drive; it went past when I turned into the parking lot. I was getting Lola her favorite yogurt and some crackers and those ginger pops for nausea, anything to settle her stomach, the morning sickness is brutal, man. So I went in and got everything Lola needed, bought some coffee beans and mango juice and my favorite local eggs."

I nodded. I shopped there too, and you always knew which farm your food came from. Everything that could be was locally sourced. *Kentucky Proud*.

"He was waiting for me when I came out of the Co-op."

I sat forward.

"He was there in the lot, maybe a hundred feet away, engine idling. *I saw him*. Not like a ghost. Like some dude in a car. Like he was . . . like he was real. It's my dad, big as life, but also dead. He made eye contact and it gave me goosebumps. And damn, you know. That's my dad, who's been dead all these years, but it's him. He always drove his car like it was a Boeing 747 or a yacht—very deliberate, very precise, both hands on the wheel. And that's exactly how it was. Sitting just so. Hands just so.

"And he was looking at me so intensely, it was scary as fuck. I dropped my bag and got my phone and took some pictures." Jesse scrolled through his phone, then handed it to me across the desk.

I flipped through six shots, some of them blurred, some of them dead-center bullseye. It was a hell of a car and a hell of a man. White Egyptian cotton shirt almost a twin to the one I had on, buttoned tight to his throat. Lines of age etched in his neck, his thin hound-dog face, blue eyes like Jesse's, and a look that was knowing. Eyes that invited you to make him happy and do what he wanted . . . or else. I felt the threat of that, just looking at the picture.

But I noticed something that I had not seen with him before. He looked thinner than he had the first time I'd seen him. He looked ill. That not-quite-there look my patients got, when they were headed down the slope of cognitive decline. He was deteriorating. Perhaps following the pattern of his death. Walking that path again and again, like manifestations so often do.

Jesse gave me a look. "I think we should exhume his grave and make sure he's really there, that's how sure I am that the man in that car is my father. Have you ever dealt with anything like this before?"

I could hear the desperation in his voice.

"Yes," I said. *No*, I thought.

"Tell him the rest, Jesse."

"There's more?"

Jesse kind of laughed. All of us did. Tension relief and it

helped. We were all on the same side now. Convinced and on the run.

"As soon as I took the pictures," Jesse said, "he started revving the engine. He was so . . . angry. Malevolent. He waved at me but it was a mean gesture. Like I knew he was furious with me, and he was saying, 'I'm coming for you, kid.' I thought . . . I thought he might hit the gas and run me down, so I got the bag in the saddle pouch, tied it down, and got on my bike to take off—no way he could catch me if I didn't want to be caught, but . . . I was hyperventilating, and thinking, 'Oh great, here comes another panic attack, and I won't be able to drive,' but that's not what happened. I had a flash of memory. Like a vision. But not of the future. Of the past. It's a dream I've been having since Lola got pregnant the first time."

"The first time? Months ago?" The timeline of the sightings and the dream was interesting. I know this was the key to everything going on, but I was a long way from figuring it out.

"Yeah."

"He told me about seeing his dad this morning," Lola said. "Right after it happened. He came home so shook up. He showed me the photos and we talked—properly talked. And that's when he told me about the dream too."

"Tell me exactly what happens in the dream and the vision, Jesse. And tell me if they are different in any way."

"No. Not different. Always exactly the same, just sometimes it goes on longer, like it's telling me more and more of the story. Like it's something I need to know. But look, I need to tell you some stuff before I share the dream with you, so you can understand."

He paused, and I nodded.

"He was just that guy, you know? He'd drive that car and chain-smoke gold Tiparillo cigars. Remember those old ads, they ran them in those old Playboy magazines? *Should a gentleman offer a lady a Tiparillo?*"

"He was also a serial cheater. On Jesse's mom." Lola's eyes were hard. "One of those men who think they're entitled, right? He worked hard, he was really successful, made a lot of money, and he deserved whatever he wanted."

"Yeah, he cheated on my mom, and didn't much want to come home to the family. We were just a weight on his shoulders. He actually said so, to guy friends, didn't care that I was in the room and heard him. We were anchors, my mom and me. Dead weight."

I nodded. Plenty of doctors like that at the hospital, male and female. High on the medical hierarchy pecking order, working long hours, and because they were doctors they deserved to do whatever they wanted. They alienated their families and years later tried to make amends with adult children who wrote them off ages ago. When you create that much distance from your family, there is rarely ever a good road back.

"So, you and I, we talked about the twin thing when I came in for tests. My brother, Frankie, he died at five months. He was always really sick; he couldn't digest his food. I guess now they call it failure to thrive. It . . . I know people say I could not possibly remember any of this stuff, but people are wrong. I remember Frankie. He was my twin. I can't really describe what that's like, but—"

"I understand as much as a non-twin can understand. I've had a lot of patients who were twins. The connection isn't just emotional. It's physical too."

"I still think of him, I still miss him, sometimes I feel like he's close." His sadness was palpable. The grief for a twin, born or unborn, long gone or recent. Deep, gripping, hard for the rest of us to understand. "Frankie." He smiled. "My mother named us for outlaws. She grew up in Midway near the Offutt-Cole Tavern. Owned by Richard Cole, father of James Cole, father of Zerelda Cole James—mother of Frank and Jesse James. They had a lot of ties to Kentucky. It was a tollgate for a while, became known as the Black Horse Tavern.

"My mom said she could feel us jumping around and playing before we were born. Frankie was born first. He was bigger. She said we used to hold hands in our crib; she put us in together or we would scream until she did. I remember . . . I know it sounds nuts, but I remember him stroking my hair. I don't know how I remember that but I do. We were mirror-image twins, right? We talked about it when you were running tests."

I nodded. Situs inversus. Jesse's internal organs were on the opposite side.

"Here's what you need to understand. My dad, you know. He never liked Frankie. I always knew that. He favored me because I was the strong one and Frankie was the weak one and he was big into survival of the fittest.

"*Failure to thrive*, my dad would say. Like Frankie had failed. Then he would grab my shoulder hard and say . . . *But I've got you. The strong one. I was the strong one too.*"

"Your father was a twin?"

"Yeah. Mirror twin like me, but his brother was never born. He just . . . it's called vanishing twin. But my dad's organs were on the wrong side too."

I nodded. A twin not thriving in the womb, dying and being absorbed. Crushing to wrap your mind around.

"Did your dad have a lot of health problems, Jesse?"

"He did as a child. Metabolic derangement." Jesse gave me an ironic smile. "But he survived and then he thrived. He used to brag about it. My father was healthy and intolerant of anybody who wasn't, including his twin brother and including Frankie. When he talked about his twin who was never born, he said he had eaten his brother alive, absorbed him in the womb. He was a son of a bitch, Dr. Archer. Competitive even before birth.

"So, my dream . . . I know you'll say it can't be real, can't be a memory, because I am remembering a time when I was a baby," Jesse said slowly. "It's about the night Frankie died. When he was five months old. *We* were five months old."

I shook my head. "It could be real. Your brother died. You'll either block it out or it won't go away."

"Yeah, exactly. I think I have blocked it out, but now it keeps coming back to me whenever I fall asleep."

"Tell me the dream."

"I'm curled up by Frankie, and he is holding my hand, and he is crying and kicking his feet, legs pulled up to his belly, and I know he feels bad, I can feel it too, it's an awful pain and it makes me cry too. And then . . . someone comes into the room. I see a shadow on the wall and I go quiet because I'm scared of the shadow. Because . . . because . . ." He shut his eyes tight. "I just figured that out. Because it means my father is in the room. He would always sing to us 'Moon River'."

Crap, I thought.

"And he's going to pick me up and leave Frankie there, screaming. Just screaming. And I don't want to leave my brother, and I know he's in pain. It's hell. Oh god, I remember it, I know it's real. But this night is different."

Jesse puts his face in his hands. "Jesus Christ, I get it. I know what happened."

He is starting to breathe hard.

"Take your time, Jesse. You can stop now; we don't have to talk about it—"

"No, no, you don't understand. This night our mother doesn't come. Usually she does and she gets Frankie and leaves me with my dad. But she doesn't come. I don't know why. And my dad, this time he doesn't pick me up. He takes my blanket. And he puts it over Frankie's face, and I'm holding Frankie's hand and he is terrified and he screams and then . . . he settles and is quiet, and he is still holding my hand. And I can hear the beat of his heart. Slower and slower until it stops. And the last thing I remember is my father, taking Frankie's hand out of mine. And he's still singing to us. He doesn't miss a beat. And that's the last thing I remember before my world goes dark. And now I get it. I understand. He killed him. My father killed my brother. For no good reason other than he just chose me. Survival of the fittest."

Lola sobbed, and he put his arms around her, but he did not cry and he did not rant. He went very still, as if a weight had lifted from his shoulders.

"And now I know. Now I remember. I think this has haunted me my whole life. They always say children love their parents, even when they do terrible things, but that's just not true. I have hated my father all of my life. Laid awake at night wondering if there was something wrong with me, for hating him like I did. If I had figured it out earlier, I would have killed that son of a bitch."

He shut his eyes tight and his shoulder sagged. "Sweet, beautiful Frankie. How could any man do such a thing? Much less a father. And I remember one other thing. Cigar smoke. Can you imagine, smoking around little babies like that?" Jesse looked at me, then at Lola. "Don't you see? It's going to happen all over again. He's going to kill Lola, he's going to kill my child, and I'm the only one he'll leave alive."

Saying it out loud and often was the smart way to go. It would go from horror to acceptance, which meant they could handle things without the paralyzing fog of fear.

"When I wake up, now, some mornings, I smell cigar smoke. So I know that he's around. And I hate that so much. I grew up with the stink of cigars in the house, in the car. After he died, my mother and I moved house just to get away from the stink; it was burrowed and ingrained into the house. So I know it's got to be him. Because it comes from nowhere. Nobody's there.

"And lately I've been waking up with the memory of dreams—that I hear his footsteps on the stairs, see him bending over Lola, peering at her. He looks angry. One time I dreamed that Lola screamed. There was a mark on her cheek like she'd been slapped, and blood running from a deep scratch, and her eye swelling up."

I looked up at her and she ran a finger on her soft unblemished cheek. "He woke up screaming. It took me a long time to convince him his father wasn't there."

"He's there," Jesse said.

I nodded. "I think you're right, Jesse. We know it's real. You sense him close, and this is part of the attack. He may have a physical presence, but this is how a haunting works with the living and the dead. They get to you. From memories, experiences, and actual presence which you feel but deny because it makes no sense. He or it wants you to be sleep deprived and scared. That makes you vulnerable for what he's going to do next."

"Yeah. Kill my unborn child. But why? He didn't come at the first pregnancy. Why this one?"

"Maybe he knew I was going to lose the baby," Lola said.

And then I understood. "Lola, have you had an ultrasound?"

"No, I don't want any tests I don't have to have. They'll do one later. If I let them."

"Do you think it's possible you're carrying twins?"

"I've wondered. Just because it runs in Jesse's family. And because I am huge already, and so sick, and you are sicker with twins."

"Not just twins. *Mirror twins*. Situs inversus. Internal organs on the opposite side. Just like Jesse and just like his dad. Because it's all about the timing with mirror twins. Like other identical twins, the embryo splits, but it happens later, nine to twelve days after conception, and that is what causes the mirroring—one twin a mirror image of the other. One will be left-handed, one right-handed, birthmarks on opposite sides, and the mirroring sometimes affects the internal organs. Think about the timing here. Your father showed up about two weeks after conception. When the split happened. That's when both of you started seeing him. You and Lola are having mirror twins. And he either wants to go after both of them, or he'll make a choice."

Lola shuddered and Jesse pulled her close. "We won't let him. I won't let him."

"I'll meet with Perry and we'll make a plan."

"We better," Jesse said. "Because I know exactly what he's going to do. Same thing he did when I was growing up. Running off my friends, my first girlfriend. My dad never loved me but he wanted me to himself. And he's scary now in a way he never was before. He's going to kill Lola, Dr. Archer. He's going to kill my wife and he's going to kill both my babies. The only choice he ever makes is me. He wants to keep me all to himself."

Lola put a hand over her face. "Jesse, I'm not going to just lay there and let it happen."

"Neither am I, but you are pregnant and vulnerable so let's not pretend different."

"We'll stop him," I said. "You have to survive this and you have to pace yourself. I know you're not sleeping. And in your place, I don't think I'd sleep much either. But hypervigilance is exhausting and the exhaustion, anxiety, and fear are likely fueling the panic attacks. When are you safe?" I asked Lola. "You're not with Jesse all day, right?"

"I'm safe teaching. I'm safe in my office, at the college, I'm safe there."

"What are you doing when she's there at EKU?"

"Working at the garage."

"Schedule some serious sleep time when she's at the college. Because you can't keep this up. And in the meantime, we'll resolve it. As best we can."

"How?"

"I think your father is possessed and has been for a really long time. Is he a terrible man? He is. But I think he also opened himself up to something dark and deadly, and I think killing your brother was his first step in that direction. Whatever it was would welcome that. It could have already taken him over. So we will track his physical presence, figure out where he goes and when, what draws him, and then we'll do an exorcism. And be ready. With something like this, it's going to be a series of exorcisms, and it will get worse before it gets better."

"Why is that?" Lola asked.

"Because an exorcism pisses it off."

"It being my father or it the dark entity thing?"

"Both."

Jesse nodded. "I think he will for sure be there on the opening night of *Bad Dad Tango*. Even if nobody else will be."

I shook my head at him. "Best to end this way before then." In a perfect world. "Let me get with Perry and Chloe. We'll put together a plan. In the meantime, stay safe, stay together, and stay in touch."

This one was a phenomenon on steroids. A codependent obsession from a father who was possessed . . . and dead.

TEN

The camera on Lola and Jesse's balcony started recording at seven eighteen p.m., tripped by the blur of a man on the railing. If it had been set up for sound, you could have heard Lola scream. You would have heard the screech of her cat, Virginia Kitty, who was on the attack.

People were finishing dinner, walking their dogs, and a neighbor heard the screams. At least two of them called the police. Both of them saw Jesse arrive after the screams. None of them saw his father.

Erebus Lynch can be seen quite clearly in the camera recording, standing on the balcony, face pressed against the glass door that led into the living room. The door does not open, but somehow Lynch gets from the balcony, into the house, where he is attacked by an infuriated Virginia Kitty.

The first I heard of it was when my brother-in-law, Tom, a uniformed Lexington Kentucky police officer, called me about a husband who had been arrested for domestic violence. One Jesse James Lynch. His wife, the victim, Lola Strickler, was being tended to by the EMTs from Fire Station #4 which had initially answered the call of a woman injured on Hampton Court. The police were there trying to arrest Jesse. Both Jesse and Lola had begged them to call me, but the officer on scene had not seen fit to summon a neurosurgeon. But my brother-in-law gave me a call, a colleague had told him my name had come up, and he figured I'd want a heads-up.

"You say injured. How bad?"

"The wife? OK, but she's bruised and there's a pretty deep scratch on her cheek. It was bleeding pretty bad but she refused to go to the ER."

I was on my way home from the hospital, so I made a turn on South Broadway and headed that way. Thinking about the scratch on her cheek. Another one of Jesse's dreams. It could have been a vision, an intuition. Or he could have made it come true. Except I had the video, which put Jesse in the clear.

The police officer who responded, a crew-cut redhead with tired brown eyes, had Jesse sitting in the grass by the curb. A sure sign that he was about to be handcuffed and arrested. Lola stood next to him, arms folded, a red gash on her cheek seeping blood. She wore an oversized bloodstained sweatshirt and yoga pants and her Reeboks. Her left cheek where she'd been gouged was swelling and she'd have a black eye by morning. She'd been hit pretty hard. I had to take a breath or two in the car to calm down. Then I was out and heading toward Jesse and Lola.

"Dr. Archer," she shrieked, running in my direction. "Tell them Jesse didn't do this. Don't let them take him to jail."

Officer Merch, with the brown eyes, stepped in front of me. "Excuse me, sir, please go back to your car."

"Of course. I'm a doctor though, and with your permission I'd like to look at Lola's cheek."

"Are you the neurosurgeon she wanted me to call?"

"Yes."

"Does she need a neurosurgeon, sir?"

I sighed. "There is a camera screwed into the porchlight on the balcony where Lola's attacker was waiting for her. It's linked to my phone. Would you like to see it?"

He glanced at his partner. Blonde ponytail. She was watching Lola with the exasperation law enforcement feels when women protect the husband who has hurt them. She was young enough not to understand the reasons a woman might do that.

Merch put out his hand for my phone, which I held tight to.

"Sorry, there is confidential patient information on the phone. Let me text you this, OK?"

He nodded. No problem. Everything was caught on video these days, and it sure as hell made his job easier.

He watched it. Frowning. Looked at Lola, who held an ice pack to her cheek. The EMTs had been looking after her. "Do you know this guy on the balcony?"

"Well, it's not my husband, so please let him go."

"Ma'am, he is not yet in custody."

"He didn't hurt me. The guy on the video is the one who attacked me."

"Do you know who he is?"

She waved a hand. "Yes."

The officer waited. "Ma'am?"

"My husband's father. Erebus Lynch. That's the man who came in through the balcony."

"Was the door unlocked or did he force his way in?"

"He . . . I guess you could say he forced his way in."

"Through an unlocked door."

"It was locked."

"Did he break the glass, ma'am?"

"No."

"But the door was locked."

"Yes."

"Maybe you left it open a crack?"

"It was locked. I keep it locked."

He nodded. "And you've made police reports about this guy before?"

"Yes. Exactly. My husband didn't do this. He's not the man in the video."

Merch nodded. "Since you know this man, he's your father-in-law. Can you give me his location? Address? Phone number?"

"No. I don't know that information," Lola said softly.

"But his name is Erebus Lynch, father of Jesse James Lynch?"

"That's correct."

"If you're OK, ma'am, if you'll just hang tight, I need to run this." He gave his partner a look. He didn't believe a word of it, and she nodded, staying close to Jesse, who looked over at Lola. Who headed over to him.

"Ma'am," the woman officer said. "I'll need you to stay where you are."

Lola looked at me, and we moved away. "What now?"

"Get a lawyer. Jesse hasn't been arrested, but they want him, and they're looking for probable cause. You got somebody?"

"Let me call Ray. He'll know what to do." She moved away, talking softly.

Merch went to his partner, and they were talking in a huddle. I looked at Jesse. He nodded. I waved. This was utterly surreal. Even for me.

They had him up on his feet, putting him in handcuffs.

"What are you doing?" I asked, keeping my distance. They didn't like how things were unfolding and I didn't blame them.

Merch gave me a hard look. "Did you think it was funny? To show me that video? It's obviously a fake. Which could get you charged with obstruction of justice."

"You'll have to prove it's a fake. Because it's not."

"Seriously? This is Erebus Lynch. He's Jesse's father. He's been dead for eighteen years. Can you explain that?"

I shook my head. No point in trying.

"Call Ray," Jesse shouted to Lola.

"On it," she said. She hung up. Stayed dry-eyed and angry while Jesse was put in the back of the police car. "This is fucking surreal."

"Tell me everything that happened, Lola. Wait, let me drive you home, make sure you get there safe."

"But Jesse—"

"You called his stepfather, right? Let him take care of Jesse. Let's get you home."

ELEVEN

I went into Lola's house first, and she trailed behind me, afraid to go inside.

"You sure you want to stay here?" I asked.

"Ray said he'd get Jesse home to me tonight. If Ray says so, it happens."

I did a walk-through of the condo, it was clear and light, nothing dark there. Virginia Kitty rubbed up against my leg and let me pet her. A first for me.

Lola ran across the room and picked her up, and the cat put both paws around her neck and made little mewing noises. "Oh, baby, my sweet Virginia, I thought he might have hurt you." Lola looked at me over her shoulder. "But she looks fine, doesn't she?"

"She looks great. Cats are actually quite good with this sort of thing." I reached out and risked stroking Virginia and she began to purr.

"She likes you," Lola said.

The couch cushions were across the room, one torn and shedding fluff. Lola picked the pillow up and sat with it in her lap, laying Virginia on top like the queen she was. "Baby gets a pillow," Lola said, then looked at me.

I took the chair by the fireplace. "Tell me everything."

"So it was late, past supper time, and I was excited about the babies, and hungry but too sick to eat. Jesse was working late, and I'd fallen asleep on the couch, when Virginia Kitty shrieked and woke me up. She was climbing up the curtains on the balcony doors, hissing and spitting. As soon as I woke up, I heard him singing, 'Moon River'. I saw the shape of a man, like a dark shadow, looking in through the window. It was him. Virginia Kitty was doing this deep-chested growl howl she does, and I grabbed my phone and called Jesse—I mean, he wasn't even home yet, and then . . . and then it . . ." She trailed off, frowning.

"I saw a flash of light and he was right there inside the house, just there, I don't even get how. The door was still shut but somehow he just got in, and he was right there. Jesse's father. Then another flash of light, and he was right next to me, inches away this time, and I screamed and his mouth opened in a scream too, only no sound came out. But it was like he was mocking me."

Her voice went low and matter of fact as she carried on telling her story. There'd been yet another flash of light and she was knocked backward, scratched across the cheek, and she hit the floor. The cat landed on his shoulder and bit him. Jesse, who was already headed home when she called, arrived then—she knew because she heard the engine of the Ducati. She'd scrambled up off the floor and tried to run, and she didn't even see him move, but he was right there in front of her, and she got hit again. The next thing she remembered was Jesse lifting her onto the couch. And she was crying so hard she could barely tell him what had happened.

"And then the EMTs came in, and the police, because some of the neighbors heard me screaming. And they took Jesse outside and . . ." She put her face in her hands.

"They tried to get me to go to the ER, only because I'm pregnant, which everyone seems to think is a medical condition. The last thing I needed was a long wait and medical bills. Not for a scratch on my face."

"Keep it disinfected," I told her. "Those kinds of bites and scratches can get infected easily."

"Bites?" she echoed with such a look of horror that I was sorry I'd brought it up.

Lola leaned close. "Dr. Archer, I know why Erebus was here today of all days. My doctor called. She was able to fit me in for an ultrasound this morning, a cancellation, because after saying no to an early test, I wanted one fast, for obvious reasons." She gave me a worried smile. "Two heartbeats. One twin hiding behind the other. One placenta and one sac."

"Which means the egg divided late in the embryonic process. So you have identical twins, and a likelihood that they're mirror twins. Congratulations on your babies, Lola."

"I wish I could enjoy this without being so scared."

"I've talked to Perry. He thinks we should move up the timeline and do a house protection blessing and ritual tonight. For your safety. But I know you're exhausted, so if it's too much, just say so."

"Is it awful?"

"Not at all. I think you'll be charmed."

"And we can't do an exorcism on the house?"

"No, it doesn't work that way. Erebus Lynch is the target, not the house. If we can pin him down, we can try and exorcise the entity inside him—on the porch, in the house, wherever he is. But the house is not the problem. The house is full of happiness and light. So the next step is a house blessing and protection ritual. To try and keep him out."

"Will that work?"

"Perry says it will."

Lola said, "It would be good to feel safe in my home again."

We heard the front door open, then footsteps in the hallway and Jesse's voice calling for Lola. Jesse went straight to her when he entered the room, wrapping her in his arms. He was followed by another man, olive complexion, dark curly hair going very grey. Deep-socketed brown eyes, and the ease of a man with confidence to burn.

"You must be Dr. Archer," he said. He shook my hand. "I'm Ray, Jesse's stepfather. I can't thank you enough for everything you've done."

"Is Jesse in the clear?" I asked.

Ray looked up with a bit of a smile. "Oh yes, I've seen to that. But there's a complication."

"Which is?"

Jesse grinned. "They think your video is real after all. Some neighbor recorded Dad on the balcony, and he turned to face them, so it's clearly the same guy we got off the balcony camera. *My dad. My dear dead dad.* Of course, they ran him through the database and found his death certificate. That didn't go over well. They decided it was a misidentification. So they're still looking for the perpetrator."

"And that will be their problem if they find him. I'll tell my brother-in-law, Tom, a fellow cop, so he can give them the heads-up on how dangerous he is."

"The main thing is that Jesse is in the clear." Ray gave me an ironic smile. "Jesse tells me you like his Ducati motorcycle. Do you like the local Ducati bourbon?"

"I do."

"Good man." He went to the kitchen, and I heard the chink of glasses and he came back with two tumblers of amber liquid. "I run the Ducati Distillery. This is something new. Would you give it a try and tell me what you think? Kids, have you had anything to eat? I'm ordering in. You'll join us, won't you, Dr. Archer?"

"Actually," Lola said. "We are having a very special ceremony tonight, and I would be grateful for all of you to stay, eat whatever Ray orders, and be here for that."

Ray gave me a look. "Pardon me for being inquisitive, but will this be an exorcism? Some kind of big dramatic affair with flying furniture and screams and howls like in the movies? I'm happy to stay and help if I can, I just want to know what to expect."

"It's a blessing and protection ritual for the home. It's spiritual and rather beautiful," I explained.

"Even better," Ray said, raising his glass. "I knew Erebus Lynch most of his life, and I have not been happy to renew the connection. If you're confident the ceremony will help, I'd appreciate it if you and your colleagues would consider doing the same at my home too. I think my beautiful Lavee would sleep all the better. Because otherwise the only option seems to be just letting Erebus Lynch do any damn thing he wants. I would shoot the man, but evidently he'd only come back again." He gave me his most charming smile. "It's never easy, is it?"

I couldn't read Ray on this. He was being flippant, as if it was all a joke, but happy to go forward with whatever we wanted. Humoring us. And yet. He did not seem to doubt that Erebus was a genuine presence. He knew things. And was keeping them to himself.

I raised my glass. "No, Ray, it's never easy. But hey, thank God for bourbon."

"Do you like it?"

"Very much."

"I'll have a bottle or three delivered to your house. No, no, don't turn me down. It will be my pleasure. If there's anything I can do to help with . . . with all of this, just let me know. I'm afraid it's a bit over my head, so I leave it in your capable hands."

"Actually, Ray, there is one thing you can do. Would you ask your wife if we could set up a time to talk? I'd like her insight on a few things. I can have my office manager call her and set something up. Where is she anyway? I thought she'd be here."

Ray gave me a sideways smile and grimace. "Things are a little tense now between Lola and Lavee. But I'm sure she'll be happy to meet with you. To be honest, I've been trying to hold her off. But if that's what you really want—"

"It is."

"Brave man. No doubt you want to know all the juicy secrets about her husband, whose ghost appears to have risen from the grave to cause just as much havoc as the bastard did when he was alive?"

"Just the ones I need to know. I take it you know him rather well."

"Oh, yes, I know the son of a bitch. But I don't know the secrets." And he gave me a smile that said otherwise.

TWELVE

Perry and Chloe didn't live far down the road, so they arrived quickly when I called them.

Chloe and Lola embraced. "Have you told them about the babies yet?" Chloe asked.

"Just Noah. And Jesse was there, of course," Lola said.

"You should," Chloe said. "And remember. I'll be coming by daily for a while to take readings. We'll know if this is working. I'll find the trail if Erebus is around. My guess is that after the ritual I'll still find his presence outside the house, but he won't be able to get in. If it was anybody doing the ritual other than my husband, I'd say you had a fifty-fifty chance of it working that well. But with Perry doing it—the odds are way in your favor."

Lola huddled with Chloe a bit longer, then Lola looked up and raised her voice. "I want to thank all of you for being close during these weird and terrifying days. And I am honored to have you here as we do the blessing and protection ritual for our home. Before we begin, I have some amazing news which will likely *not* come as a surprise to some of you." She smiled at Jesse, who crossed the room to stand behind her. "I had an ultrasound this morning. *Two* heartbeats, and a side view of one of our babies, with the other barely visible, hiding behind her sister. Five or six months from now we will all be welcoming twin daughters into the family. I have one of those grainy, hard-to-figure-out ultrasound screenshots of the babies to share with you—yes, thank you, Ray, if you would pass that around."

"Thank you for inviting everyone to stay for the blessing," Ray said. "And letting me be part of this." He leaned close and kissed her gently on the cheek. "Congratulations on the babies. Our beautiful family grows."

* * *

I had never been to a house blessing before, and it was the opposite of an exorcism. It was a gathering in, not a casting out. It was a celebration of the home and an invitation to light and peace and happiness, with a warding off of anything dark.

Perry, in neatly pressed khakis and a Mediterranean blue dress shirt, no longer in the dark heavy robes he's worn in the past, lit the candles he had placed at the balcony door, the front door, and a window in every room. He lit a smudge stick and left a trail of sweet grass smoke in every room. We stood in a messy huddle, watching, and he asked us to repeat the words that he said.

His voice, resonant and full of inexplicable power, followed by the shy murmur of the rest of us, following along.

"We gather here in this sweet, sweet home of Lola and Jesse Lynch, where their two tiny children, yet unborn, will be welcomed with love. Keep them safe here. Let the winds of heaven blow the darkness away, and come softly to keep them safe. We celebrate the light and the love of this home, and ask for harmony, good fortune, and the bright white light of protection. We open the house to joy and to love, and we ward off all harm, by turning it back upon itself. We raise our glasses in celebration of this beautiful home." Chardonnay for some, mango juice for others, and bourbon shared round.

After the ritual was complete, Perry quietly went round and blew out the candles, and I watched all of them. Happy, hopeful, as if we had all been blessed along with the house. And it came to me, as it always does, what an extraordinary man Perry Cavanaugh was, and the depths he could draw on. This was not about pretty words as much as it was about the man who said them, and the centered power of his presence and his voice.

Perry had never been a rule follower. He had a spiritual integrity that never wavered—a strong faith, a gentle heart and the courage of a warrior. He'd turned away from organized religion while teaching at an exorcist symposium at the Vatican, where he came face to face with the darkness that was the church. God is woven into all things, he'd told me. The darkness and the light.

I knew the blessing would work. I had faith in Perry's powers.

Lola and her babies would be safe inside their own home from now on. But I didn't think it the time or the place to point out that we hadn't dealt with the problem—not by a long shot.

It was possible that keeping Erebus out would do nothing more than make him even angrier.

And Lola couldn't stay inside the safety of the house forever.

THIRTEEN

I had mixed feelings when Jesse's mother tracked me down while I was having a late lunch at Pies & Pints. I'd made the incorrect assumption that she and Joyce, my office manager, would agree on an appointment time and I would see her at the office on Manchester Street, at a time that was mutually convenient and when I was prepped and ready. Not now when I had a large pizza with everything, and a pitcher of very cold beer. My lunch was dinner time for normal people. I had call blocking engaged, but not the silencing, because Moira and the boys were up the street at Rupp Arena for Disney on Ice, a much beloved tradition for my boys. My oldest, Marcus, rated it second only to the My Little Pony conventions. He was a die-hard Brony, and he planned to be a cop when he grew up, like Moira's brother, Tom. I could picture his heavy belt with all the cop stuff strapped to his waist and a My Little Pony holstered with his gun. Bronies are Bronies for life.

But for my youngest? Disney on Ice was number one, and Vaughn had replaced soccer practice with skating lessons which were easier to fit into our schedule.

Friday in downtown Lexington is fun. Bright lights, shows at Rupp and the Opera House, more and more tourists as the city got featured in the *Southern Living* top ten cities again and again. I tried not to think about how badly things had gone for Austin when they got discovered. How Nashville had become the end point for what looked like half of LA. I didn't blame people for wanting to live there—Nashville was cool. And no matter what the locals will tell you, the traffic was hell before the Hollywood exodus.

In truth, I liked the happy energy visitors brought as they wandered through the Distillery District, went to basketball games, toured the horse farms, went to Keeneland racetrack,

Comic-Con, and the annual Halloween Thrillerfest, where the city offered free dancing lessons so anybody who wanted could join in the dancing zombie parade. My take is if you want to move here, come on down.

I was watching the door for my wife and kids when I saw a woman walk through, her attention immediately locking in on me.

Five-eight or nine, thick, silver-streaked chestnut hair, soft knee-high boots in brandy leather, boyfriend jeans, and a thick crew-neck black sweater. A string of fat white pearls hung to the waistband of her jeans.

She looked expensive, elegant. She caught my eye with the masterful ease of a woman who is used to male attention, and gave me a steady look that assumed I was already under her spell as she walked straight to my table, her boot heels clicking on the old wood floors.

"I'm Lavinia Lynch—Jesse's mom. Everybody calls me Lavee. Your office manager left me a message that you wanted to make an appointment to talk to me. This afternoon worked for me but she said you were unavailable." She raised an eyebrow.

I sipped my beer and was gratified by the pink flush of annoyance as she cocked her head to one side.

"Why did she say you were unavailable?" she demanded.

"This is what unavailable looks like for me. I'm having a cold beer and some private dude time watching a basketball game. My wife and kids are on their way to join me after Disney on Ice."

"Well, here I am. With everything going on, it seemed like an emergency to me."

I didn't ask her how she found me. I didn't want to know. I admit she had a point.

"Please, sit. Let me share my pizza and get you something to drink."

"No, thanks, but I appreciate the offer." She gave me a grim look. "I'm sure Jesse and Lola have told you everything about Erebus. What a terrible father and husband he was. And they'd be right. Ray said the police considered exhuming his body to see if he faked his own death, but now they've changed their mind and decided to run with 'unknown attacker'."

"Can't say I blame them so long as they leave Jesse alone."

"Ray has seen to that."

She and Ray had money. They knew people. For Jesse's sake, I was glad.

"Ray and I talked it over and we decided you need to know everything. Confidentially."

"Of course."

"And I'm here not just to give information." She lowered her voice. "I have *physical evidence* of what is going on with Erebus. So maybe you can figure out what the hell is going on with him, because I have to say that even though I know a lot, I'm still . . . baffled. And I have the very annoying feeling I'll be looking over my shoulder to see if he is behind me for the rest of my life if you can't help. I'm hoping you can find a way out for all of us."

"I can see why you'd feel that way. What kind of physical evidence are you talking about?" I asked carefully.

She gave me a nod. "Yeah, good question. And if it sounds like I'm describing a crime scene, let me tell you, Jesse's father was a walking crime scene all of his life. And evidently still is after his death. If you have an explanation for that, I'd love to hear it."

"I'm working on it. You have any theories?"

"Nothing that really makes any sense. So. Let me tell you what I know and give you what I've got, and you can take it from there." She placed a baggie on the table. "I've been finding these outside my house for the last three months, give or take. The kind of white Tiparillo cigar butts he used to smoke and . . . and evidently *still* does." She held up a baggie of smoked cigar ends and shook them at me. "I gathered some of them up and used that DNA testing lab in Louisville."

I sat forward. "When do you get the results?"

"I already got them, that's why I'm here. It's Erebus, all right. His DNA, no question, including signs of the lung cancer that killed him, and his issues as a mirror twin. His DNA results are weird. They can tell from the DNA if you're alive or dead."

"I know. Which is it?"

She set the envelope on my table. "*Both.*"

I thought about that.

"I have one other thing to give you. And I apologize in advance for how gruesome it is."

"Gruesome doesn't sound good."

"No," she said. "It doesn't."

She pulled out a chair and sat. She was an odd mix of vulnerability and resilience. She gave me a quick half-smile that showed the hint of a dimple. "And I'm sorry I interrupted your dude time, but after what happened last night, I thought we should talk soon. This kind of physical escalation seems dangerous to me. This stalking Lola and watching her sleep. Jesse's exhausted."

"They both are." I didn't tell her about Jesse's panic attacks. That was Jesse's business. "I wanted to ask you about a dream Jesse keeps having."

She frowned. "A dream?"

"Or a memory. Or a vision. It's hard to tell. I figured you could help me sort it."

"What is it?"

"It's about Frankie. The night he died."

She froze.

"I'm sorry—"

"No, no, please. Tell me. If it's upsetting Jesse, I need to know. They were so beautiful together, those boys. I know he was so little when Frankie died, but I don't think Jesse ever got over it. I know I didn't."

"How did he die, Mrs. Lynch?"

"He had metabolic disorder, and couldn't keep enough food down to thrive. He was wasting away, nothing was helping, and one night he just went to sleep and didn't wake up."

"Did you find him in his crib? Can you tell me how it played out?"

"Why? What did Jesse tell you?"

"Let me tell you his dream," I said. And, as gently as I could, I did.

She shut her eyes tight as she listened and worked hard to

hold back tears. When I had finished, I handed her a napkin and she wiped her eyes and leaned forward.

"It does not make sense to me that a five-month-old baby could know—or remember—what happened to his brother. But. Some of the details are exactly right. I always went to comfort Frankie when he was crying, but that one night Erebus insisted he would go—and I let him. I've never spoken about that to anyone before—I blamed myself for years, wondering whether if I'd been the one to soothe my crying child, I would have seen the signs that these weren't ordinary tears, that I needed to ring an ambulance before it was too late. How could Jesse know that? It doesn't make sense," she repeated, sounding lost.

"You never discussed it with Jesse? You're sure?"

"Never. But what you're telling me is that Erebus killed my son." She put her head in her hands, thinking.

"Did the doctors say Frankie died of metabolic disorder?"

She shook her head. "It made him vulnerable. He was wasting away and we were trying one thing after another to turn that around. But the death certificate said sudden infant death syndrome—which makes sense if Erebus . . . if Erebus did that to him. Put a blanket over his face . . ." She pulled the sleeves of her sweater down until they completely covered her hands.

"What exactly do you think happened?" I asked.

"I think . . . it's just that Erebus was so odd that night. Going into the nursery, when Frankie was screaming . . . Usually he would pick Jesse up, if the babies were crying, and just leave Frankie there on his own to cry. Of course I would go right in to get Frankie, but it was infuriating. I hated him for it. I still do. But that night he was so insistent that he would take care of both boys, and Frankie soon stopped crying . . . Then Erebus brought him to me, wrapped in a blanket, and he was . . . Look, I'm sorry, I can't talk about this. Frankie was so sweet. He was such a little love. If Erebus killed him—"

"Do you think he did?"

She thought about it. "Yes. I do."

I picked up the pitcher and poured her a beer, and she took it shyly. Not a beer drinker. I put a slice of pizza on a plate and pushed it across the table.

"Oh no . . ."

"This is the South, Mrs. Lynch, and I can't eat if you don't eat, and I'm hungry."

She tilted her head to one side. "So you're local?"

"Born and raised."

"Me too. Grew up in Midway."

"Jesse told me. Related to the famous James family of outlaws."

She took a reluctant sip of beer, leaving a lipstick mark on the side.

I took a large bite of pizza, refilled my glass.

She took a small bite of pizza, then wiped her mouth. "I guess we can't prove any of this, but we don't actually need to. Knowing is enough. I can't believe Jesse . . . Such a crushing thing for him."

"For both of you. I'm so sorry."

She nodded. Took a breath. "OK. Now, onto the thing I wanted to tell you about. And one other thing I want to give you."

"The gruesome thing?"

"Yes." She paused.

"It . . . it's kind of shocking." She shut her eyes tight. "Jesse's father has come back—and not just in spirit."

"What do you mean? Come back from where?"

"Come back from the dead, Dr. Archer. I'm not talking about going over the bridge to Cincinnati. I'm talking about . . . *resurrection*."

"This is a haunting, Mrs. Lynch. I think your husband was possessed before he died and his ghost—"

"He isn't a ghost. But I do think he was very dark before he died. He got worse over the years, that's for sure. But he did die, I did have him buried, and he did come back."

"How can you be so sure this is what's going on? That this is a resurrection?"

"Because this isn't the first time this has happened."

FOURTEEN

"What? That doesn't make any sense."

According to Lavee, her late husband Erebus Lynch had died and been resurrected—and this wasn't the first time. I was an old hand at ghosts and possessions, but even to someone like me, her story seemed implausible.

Lavee sighed. "I get your reaction but here's what I *know*, Dr. Archer. You're free to come to your own conclusion. I would *welcome* another explanation. But fact: Erebus died of lung cancer when Jesse was fourteen. I sold the house and Jesse and I moved in with Ray, who has a great place in the Distillery District. When Jesse was nineteen, going to the University of Kentucky, playing guitar, learning how to tango, riding motorcycles with Ray and having the time of his life . . . I saw my ex-husband in traffic, following me in his old gold Caddy."

The Caddy again. A chill went up my spine.

"Then I started finding those cigar tips near my car, and on the rooftop patio of our townhouse—Ray is a master distiller and I run the business side of our small-batch bourbon distillery—Ducati Heat."

"So he'd been inside your house without you knowing?"

"Yeah. Sound familiar? For all I know he was watching me sleep just like he was with Lola. And then Erebus started calling me on the phone." She glanced up. "Have you ever heard of anything like that?"

I nodded. "Phone calls from the dead are a known phenomenon. But the only cases I'm familiar with are calls from family members getting in touch after death, to say they are OK, to say they love you, to give comfort when they think it's needed."

"Erebus only worries about himself, dead or alive. And he always called when I was alone."

"What did he say?"

She narrowed her eyes, shivered. "He didn't talk; he sang to me. 'Moon River'."

"Jesse said his father was singing that when he came into the room and killed Frankie."

"Jesus. Yes. He was singing it when he brought Frankie out of the nursery and handed him to me."

"Why 'Moon River'? Do you know?"

"It was kind of his theme song. He loved the movie with Audrey Hepburn but always thought the ending was crap because she stayed behind for some man when she really wanted to leave. He would always shout, 'Run, Audrey, run,' all through the movie. It was annoying as hell."

Moira and I had an ongoing argument about that. I wanted Audrey to stay but Moira always said she should go.

"For a while I thought that no one saw Erebus but me, and maybe I was just . . . imagining it, my worst nightmare, right? Maybe losing my mind. And I didn't tell a soul, not even Ray. Then one day Jesse said he saw a gold Cadillac just like his dad's. That's what made me decide I had to deal with it."

"What did you do?"

She raised her chin. "Erebus showed up one night. He came into the garage as I was getting out of my car. I defended myself. With . . . with a chainsaw. Ray has all kinds of tools in there and it was hanging on the wall, and I . . . I never used one before and they're hard to control, and it kind of jumped when Erebus was reaching for me, and it cut off his hand."

I gave her a sideways look. *Kind of jumped?* Except I know from experience that they do. And if you haunt people and scare them, you get what you get.

"The blood was . . ." She was looking very white around the lips. "He bled out on the floor of the garage, and I . . . I called Ray. By the time he got there, Erebus was dead again, no question. We rolled him into a carpet, put him in the trunk of Ray's car, and dumped him."

"Where?"

"The same place we buried him. If you're going to get rid of a body, that makes the best sense. It was Ray's idea. He's good in an emergency.

"When we got back to the house after dumping the body . . . his hand was still there on the floor of the garage. We'd left it behind, in all the blood and panic."

She dug in her very large purse and slid a Styrofoam box sealed with tape and set it on the table. "It's been kept frozen and it's wrapped in dry ice to keep it cold."

"You kept his hand?"

She took a deep breath. "I thought I might have it analyzed one day. Then I realized that I couldn't just wander into the police station or a DNA lab with a dismembered body part and walk back out again."

"No argument there."

I saw the dimple again, and there was a part of me that could not believe we were having this conversation.

"But I kept it because I thought it would come in useful someday. As it has. Erebus is regenerating somehow, that's my own theory. Are you familiar with mirror science?"

"Not much."

"Study up," she said.

I looked at the package.

"I can take it back home to the freezer if—"

"No," I said, putting a firm hand on the box. "I have somebody I want to take a look at this."

"I thought you might. And no, before you ask, I do not want it back. I never want to see it again." She scooted her chair back. "Your wife will be here in five minutes, give or take, so I'll head out."

"She's got another twenty before the show ends."

"She's already on her way."

"Why do you say that?"

"I know things." She gave me a sassy little smile, scooped up the slice of pizza I had given her, tossed her head and walked away. I watched her the whole way to the door but she didn't turn back.

And as she went out, Moira and my boys came thundering in.

My three reasons for not riding a Ducati.

FIFTEEN

Dr. Chloe Donatello, cutting-edge quantum biologist, and Enlightenment Project consulting biologist on staff, had called us all in for an early-morning meeting. An early-morning *emergency* meeting. She'd never done that before. The majority of her professional life involved high-level, *out-there* quantum research fueled by massive grants. The EU, which had something of a business presence in Kentucky, was funding her work with a climate-change initiative where she was putting together a tracking protocol that would identify exactly who was polluting where and how. She was also getting funding from the Department of Defense, and, at last count, the universities of Duke, Emerson and Vanderbilt—universities which did not yet require students to be the progeny of billionaires or celebrities. Governments and academic institutions came to *her*—much to the routine and malevolent envy of academic colleagues. University politics and hospital politics had one thing in common—both were hell.

Chloe worked alone and with students, deciding early on in her career that colleagues were more trouble than they were worth, and she enjoyed securing funding for her grad students and launching them into careers.

We were meeting this morning because it was one of those Saturdays when I wasn't on call and supposedly had the day off. Maybe a hospital check late in the afternoon—I had a patient I was worried about. She was fighting hard. She wanted to live. I didn't like her chances.

For now, it was all hands on deck. All hands meaning me, Chloe, and Perry. Perry had helped Moira and me adopt our sons, and I looked to him like I would a big brother. My thinking was that we needed to find a way to have Perry come face to face with Erebus Lynch. It would take an experienced exorcist like Perry, who had the gravitas and who knew the darkness, feared the darkness, and fought the darkness.

And he could grill a steak like nobody's business, as long as he had a Beefeater martini in hand.

They had fallen madly back in love again when we'd brought Chloe on board to help us track a dark entity of breathtaking malevolence who hunted humans . . . and hunted them well.

There is no love more passionate than finding your way back.

And I was ten minutes early for our meeting, which would be held on the fourth floor of the old distillery warehouse where the Enlightenment Project office was situated. There we held exorcisms and did research. It was where we had our own medical lab which included a machine for MRIs, where we hung out for brainstorming, and healed those who were haunted by darkness. Patients were treated here, but in general, we didn't want people traipsing through.

This was our first run-in with something dead coming back to life.

And I didn't like where this was going.

I also didn't like the looks of the youngish dude in the parking lot in front of the Ukrainian coffee shop, Cafe Breve, that was on the bottom floor of our building. Muscular arms folded across his chest, thick black hair short on the sides and collar length, an angular, sun-worn face, and hardness behind the tight smile, a confident, uncompromising presence. He worried me.

The parking lot was mostly empty because it was early. By late morning it would be a zoo. It was a hot spot in the Distillery District where you could get Godfather's pizza, high-end tacos, grab a burger while throwing axes, eat at Halligans—the fireman-themed cafe which had a rather creepy mannequin dressed in full firefighter gear including an air-purifying respirator out front. My dog Tash had barked her head off the first time she saw it.

You could also get Wild Bird cider, locally made, and wander through the occasional markets that set up shop selling home-baked dog biscuits (Tash preferred the peanut butter ones), handmade jewelry, children's clothes, homemade jams and jellies, and canvases from up-and-coming artists.

Better than online shopping because you could get a beer.

The dude was holding a cardboard box with the Cafe Breve logo that held coffees, bagels, and the kind of coffee cake Chloe lived for. He was leaning against the hood of a government-issue Chevrolet Tahoe SSV—Special Services Vehicle. Designed for off-road operations, high-speed pursuits, and hauling groceries. V8 engine, decked out for massive towing, which made me wonder what he towed. The stripe down the side had a shield but did not say POLICE. I was thinking NSA or FBI, but the logo said AARO.

And whoever he was, the Tahoe was thick with dust, dinged up, back fender dented and tires caked with dried mud. This was no office wonk. I had no idea what AARO was but this could not be good.

We locked eyes.

"Dr. Noah Archer?" he said. His voice was deep but easy-going-friendly, not the official monotone of intimidation. He was handling me.

"Who's asking?"

This brought him up straight. He put the box of coffees on the hood of his car and pulled a badge out of his pocket. He seemed amused when I took my time studying it.

Agent Liam Katani of AARO, All-Domain Anomaly Resolution Office, Department of Defense. I frowned.

"UFO hunters," he said. "Among other things. Anything weird comes up, they call us. We're UAP now. Officially—we operate across multiple mediums of the surrounding environment, e.g. solid, liquid, gas, vacuum."

"Uh-huh. I guess that would cover it."

He gave me a lopsided smile. "I've got copies of our 2024 report on 'The historical record of U.S. Government involvement with Unidentified Anomalous Phenomena'."

So now I knew what UAP meant.

"People get a kick out of it. Let me get you one to take home to your boys," he added.

He didn't move though. He'd made the point. He knew all about me, and considering the lack of privacy these days, he would not need to have government access to know a lot. But since he did have government access, he would know that much more. Which I didn't like.

On the other hand I had met the ghost of his great grandmother on my front porch. So we were kind of even.

"I'd love a copy. My boys will be thrilled. And let me ask—are you guys having any luck reverse engineering any extraterrestrial aircrafts that have come your way?"

He put his badge away, leaned back against the door of his car, and folded his arms. He gave me a tiny sideways smile. "You'd be surprised."

"Not necessarily."

"If this is a pissing contest, dude . . ."

I nodded. It was.

"Then I will remind you that the Tennessee Vols whipped your Wildcat asses seventy-eight to sixty-five in this year's NCAA Sweet Sixteen."

"Yeah, but in January, we beat you first—seventy-eight to seventy-three in your very own Thompson-Boling Arena, where five of our players placed double figures. Just saying."

"Yeah, kind of a surprise from a team rated twelve to our eight."

"I wasn't surprised. And I was there. On the side with all the Wildcat Kentucky blue."

"Seriously? So was I. On the side with all Tennessee Vols orange."

"You're from Knoxville?"

"Undergrad UT. But my family's from Tellico, Tennessee—Overhill Country."

"Nothing sucks like a big orange."

"I'd say it sucks for you."

"Why are you here?"

"I'm here to see Chloe. She called me in. Why are *you* here?"

"Same."

SIXTEEN

Chloe and Perry greeted Liam like their long-lost son, and he gave me a smirk over his shoulder. He wanted me to know he was loved.

Just not by me.

"Best student I ever had," Chloe told me with something of an unnecessary gush.

"He bleeds orange, Chloe," I said, smirking back.

"I have a soft spot for Tennessee. And he broke my heart when he went to work for the government after he got his PhD. When he could have worked for *me*."

"How do you explain that?" I asked him.

"Too many *X-Files* reruns while I was growing up. But for you—you caught them when they *first* came out, right. Back in the day, when you were young?"

"Yep. I'm your daddy."

Chloe grinned. "Know what his name means, Noah? Katani? It's Cherokee for 'Lucky Hunter'."

He gave me a lazy look. "Go on and ask. *Are you a real Cherokee, Agent Katani*?"

"Are you a real Cherokee, Agent Katani?"

"Half and half. My father's side barely survived the ethnic cleansing people like to call the Trail of Tears. My mother's side were the Europeans who instigated the genocide."

"Sooo . . ."

"Yeah," Chloe said, gazing at him fondly. "He's complicated."

"We could have used you a couple of years ago," I said.

"According to Chloe, you can use me now."

"How so?" I asked. "What do you hunt in that Tahoe of yours?"

His face went dark. "The resurrected. The fun term is zombie."

Almost exactly what Lavinia Lynch had said.

Perry waved us to the little section of the cavernous office where we had leather couches and chairs around a coffee table. "Let's all sit down before the coffee gets cold."

But Chloe did not sit down. She paced while the rest of us sat and drank the coffee Perry handed her. "Liam is looking for Erebus Lynch."

"How does he know about Erebus Lynch?" I asked. "That information is—was—confidential."

Liam said, "Chloe is familiar with my work on the resurrected. That's why she consulted me, and I agreed to come in on this."

"You're not in on anything," I said.

"Be glad I'm here. If you're dealing with a resurrected mirror twin, you're in for a world of hurt. Let's hope you're not. It's rare. Let's not get your panties in a wad until we know for sure."

"Do not direct the word *panties* at me," I said, settling back in the most worn-out leather chair, which happened to be my favorite.

"You say that with such dignity," Liam said. "I suppose that comes with age. Oh, nice score, by the way."

"On what?"

"That severed hand."

"How did you know about that?" I asked, looking directly at Chloe.

"Again, I was called in to consult on this. Show some gratitude. You have no idea what you're doing and I, lucky for you, do."

"Let me guess. You think Erebus Lynch was resurrected?"

"It's something I've seen before. And I'd show you my scars but I don't want to get you excited."

"Why don't you show me your research instead?"

"I'm the one with the research," Chloe said. "Gather round, children, and listen up."

It was worse than I thought.

SEVENTEEN

"OK," Chloe said. "I'm going to tell you what I found, with the hand, the cigar butts, etcetera. Then I am going to turn it over to Liam. We're just speculating; he does this for a living."

"You're saying Erebus died and came back to life?" I asked. "For real?"

"Sort of," Liam said. "He died and he came back. But what came back was not the man he used to be. They are not the same, not really human. Not when they come back."

"Depends on how you define human," Chloe said. "I've run DNA tests on the hand of Erebus Lynch. On the cigar butts found outside Lavinia Lynch's condo. And what I can tell you is that Erebus Lynch is human, yes, and was human, yes, but . . . how shall I put this? He's developing in the direction of a different kind of human."

"That's called evolution," Perry said. "I am hearing a lot of science semantics but Erebus Lynch is human and we'll treat him that way."

"Easy to say. Not easy to do if you want to stay alive," Katani said.

Chloe shrugged. "Again, Perry. Semantics. When what you mean is you expect us to treat him with compassion."

He thought about that. Nodded.

"What I can tell you is that Erebus Lynch has been dead and he has been alive and what he is now is a conflation of both. He is not well. Malnourished, dehydrated, emaciated. He takes form as human but he is something else, according to his DNA, which shows there have been changes along the way.

"Point one. Mirror twins are a part of human evolution, as Perry points out, the future maybe. They are vulnerable at birth but the ones who survive, they survive *well.* And Lynch was a mirror twin, and he died, and he regenerated and came back."

She gave all of us a long look. Clocking our reaction. "It's not as wild as it sounds."

I nodded. "Stem cells trigger tissue regeneration, and salamanders regrow their tails."

Chloe rolled her eyes at me. "This is way beyond lizards. We're talking about human twins. Conjoined twins, when separated, have had astonishing results with tissue regeneration. The separated liver regenerates—the brain, the heart, not so much, so there is a much higher fatality rate with that. When antibodies are unleashed they can go rogue. That's autoimmune disease and Lynch shows signs of that."

I nodded. "That's interesting. There's a strong link between autoimmune disease and dementia."

"Makes sense," Liam said.

Chloe looked annoyed. She had trouble differentiating between a spitball session and a lecture. "Look, there is enormous fear right now about the dangers of mirror science and what is laughably referred to as the *someday scenario* of creating mirror life. A full mirror organism that is the reflection of a natural organism. That cannot be controlled, and cannot die. But that is the usual arrogance of human science. Whatever we can create in a lab can and does happen in the real world without the help of technology, while scientists dither with their Y-fronts in a wad."

"Chloe, don't direct the word Y-fronts at Noah." Katani gave me that smirk that was starting to get annoying. "You have to love her, though."

"I do. Also, Chloe, big pharma is researching this tech for cancer treatments."

"I know. My point is that mirror life already exists—mirror twins. And the powers of regeneration are real. Like you said, Noah, we're already using mirror biology in medical treatments to give cancer patients resistance to their own antibodies—otherwise the treatments have to be done again and again because the body rejects and annihilates. With a mirror version of the cancer treatment, there is no resistance.

"My take—and what Lynch proves—is that mirror life has enormous possibilities for regenerative medicine, because mirror molecules can generate tissue repair and growth. The goal is a mirror image growth factor to stimulate cell regeneration—creating organs and limbs for transplant. Basically, the possibilities are to use bio printing to create organs for transplant, stem cell regeneration, or creating 3D-printed organs from biological materials. Or, even better, and my favorite possibility—harmonics. It's called ADE—acoustic droplet ejection. The creation of transplant organs that requires no physical contact—so no risk of infection—and gives absolute precise placement."

Liam nodded. "And high cell viability because the acoustic waves do not cause so much stress on cells. It would be a hell of a thing. And listen. The odd thing is . . . the regenerated mirror twins I have tracked are highly reactive to music. It draws them, it generates emotions and that frequently morphs into anger. I'm not sure why."

I thought of my patients whose brains were worn away with Alzheimer's, ALS, Parkinson's. Patients who had traumatic brain injuries, patients whose brain tissues were swarmed by cancer. And so often they were consoled, uplifted, comforted by music. Generating emotions and memories. And sometimes those memories would overwhelm them, and the emotion would become too much.

And I thought about Erebus Lynch, calling his wife and singing "Moon River". The song he sang when he was at his most dangerous.

The song he'd sung when he murdered Jesse's twin brother—his own son.

I looked at Katani. "So, if the music draws them in and then upsets them—"

"Not upsets," he said. "*Rage*. Like a mama bear when you pick up one of her cubs. You'll be dead as soon as she gets to you. Mauled to death, torn apart. They are that dangerous."

"So the music evokes memory and emotions, and their neural pathways are damaged and they are overwhelmed, and it makes them reactive. Patients in cognitive decline, no matter what variety, have a lot of anger. This tracks."

Chloe nodded. "And the catch to mirror tech life forms created in a lab is that there is a huge risk they will replicate uncontrollably and *cause* disease."

"Like thalidomide," I said.

Perry frowned. "Tell me how that works."

Chloe pushed hair out of her eyes. She looked impatient, like she always does when the rest of us are still trying to keep up. "Thalidomide has two mirror-image forms that can have drastically different effects. One form of thalidomide, the R-enantiomer, is a sedative that relieves morning sickness in pregnant women—while the S-enantiomer is teratogenic and causes severe birth defects."

"How exactly does this apply to Erebus Lynch?" Perry asked.

Katani looked at Chloe and she nodded.

"Here is what we already know. Erebus Lynch was and is a mirror twin—specifically a situs inversus twin, where his internal organs are reverse positioned. And Lavinia Lynch, his wife, God help her, said he has come back not once, but twice."

I gave Chloe a hard look. "I see you've brought Agent Katani up to date. I don't recall being consulted on that."

She shrugged, which annoyed me. "We need him, Noah; this is dangerous stuff and he may be the only person I know about who's seen this up close and in person."

I looked at Katani. Dead serious. No smirk. "How does this tend to play out?"

He paused. There was an energy that went through him. Like horror. "I keep track of mirror twins in a database, and cross reference it with . . . violent attacks. This is rare but incredibly dangerous. Then I follow up, talk to the relatives, who are seriously traumatized by the time I get there, the ones left alive anyway. So the way it plays out is that someone they love dies, and then comes back, angry, confused, and escalating into extreme violence. From what I can tell, most burial practices make this impossible. But if the body of the mirror twin was, say, dumped in the woods, or there was a green funeral, it can happen.

"I have checked the records and Erebus Lynch was buried twenty years ago when his son Jesse was fourteen, at the Rivers of Green Memorial Sanctuary in Woodford County, Kentucky. And that means he was not embalmed, he was not buried in a concrete vault, and he was not cremated. They dug a grave three and a half feet deep, which means an eighteen-inch smell barrier, so that animals, mostly anyway, leave them alone. They're buried too deep to be worth the trouble. And there is no danger of contaminating potable water which is found seventy-five feet below the surface.

"Bodies take an average of six weeks for the majority of the soft tissue to decompose, maybe twenty years for the bones to be absorbed into the soil. The graves are marked by GPS coordinates, plat diagrams, and a physical marker, or a tree, or . . ." He shrugged. "Whatever the family wants. Lavinia Lynch had an engraved fieldstone placed to mark her husband's grave. Plots can be reused if the family wants.

"Rivers Green is managed by a land preservation group. Erebus Lynch was buried in a shroud. All of this is in the records of Rivers Green, which I accessed as soon as I talked to Chloe. Supposedly Lynch is still there. I suggest we go take a look. I'm pretty sure I know what we'll find."

"Which is?"

"No body but DNA traces of the regeneration process. Which means he is a regenerated mirror twin."

"Explain that, will you? How such a thing could be possible?" Perry said.

Katani looked at me. "You're the neurosurgeon. Why don't you take a shot? You've been thinking about it, haven't you?"

I had. The theory had been seeded when I'd first talked to Lavee. It was the only way I saw any possibility for this to happen naturally. To happen at all.

"Here's what I know," I said. "People think that when you die, the body just shuts down, but in truth, studies in post-mortem brain activity show that brain cells become more active after death. They're called zombie genes. They can function hours after the rest of the body has stopped functioning; they can grow and form new neural connections. But within approximately thirty minutes the brain structure begins to collapse and bacteria triggers decomposition. And you get autolysis—where the cell membranes break down, and release enzymes that start self-digestion. Freezing temperatures can slow it down but won't stop it. So somewhere in that process of dying, which was causing damage to his brain, Erebus Lynch started regenerating tissues."

"Enough to come back to life?" Perry asked.

"It's the only explanation I can think of. But, it comes with a lot of damage to the neurons, and that could explain why Erebus Lynch has come back to life, but he's not . . . Erebus Lynch. At least not the man he used to be."

"That's putting it mildly." Katani pulled three worn, coffee-stained manila folders out of his battered cardboard box. "Excuse the low tech here, but the only way I can keep my results confidential is not to have them in any online storage whatsoever. My cloud is your cloud. So I file my reports with only the information I want the government to know. They can't be trusted."

"Can you?" I asked.

"Here is how I *can* be trusted. I can be trusted to track Erebus Lynch and dispose of him. Properly. So he can never come back. Because let me tell you. Every single time a mirror twin regenerates, more of their brain is damaged, and they are that much more dangerous. They will be drawn to the lives they used to have, to the people they used to love, but it's like unleashing a monster on the family." He glanced over at Perry. "They come back but they come back wrong. Violent in ways you cannot imagine, so let me show you what I've seen and we'll see how sympathetic you are after you've taken a hard look. Because you might want to save your compassion for their victims. Which are always their families."

I rubbed my chin. "Listen, Katani. I treat brain-damaged patients every day and they're not serial killers and they're not monsters. Prosecutors, pseudo doctors, whatever—they've been using brain scans to try and explain and convict people and they always will. But brain damage does not necessarily mean violence."

"Think not? This kind of brain damage does. Here are some crime-scene photos for you."

Chloe finally sat down on the leather couch beside Perry, and I held my tongue as Liam Katani prepared to do his dog-and-pony show.

It hadn't escaped my notice that when I'd asked Katani flat out if I could trust him, he'd dodged the question with the skill of a practiced politician.

EIGHTEEN

The crime-scene photos were impressive and not in a good way.

Katani laid out a photo on the coffee table and tapped on it. The image was of a male, human, age impossible to determine, face torn off, one leg neatly stacked next to the other, neither attached. A big guy. A river of blood, my guess would be twelve pints for a guy that size. Dried pools of dark, black red.

"It looks like an animal attack," Chloe said.

"It was. That is the point I am trying to make." Liam gave her a fond look. I had a feeling that his student–professor crush burned strong. "If a mountain lion wanders into an elementary school, you take it down if you're smart. Grizzlies who develop a taste for hikers get hunted down. You can agree with that or disagree, but that is what this is. These regenerates are too dangerous to live. And when you hunt them and kill them, you have to kill them for real."

"Which means?" Perry said.

"Incineration. If Lavinia Lynch had cremated her husband, she wouldn't be in this mess."

Katani started laying more photos on the table, making them snap as he laid them out one by one. "All of these victims share one trait—they were killed by a member of the family, a situs inversus twin, who had died within the last year. So while brain injury may not guarantee violent behavior, brain regeneration, after autolysis *does*. I've got the test results to back that up."

I looked up. "Chloe?"

She nodded.

The photos were a nightmare.

Perry took one look and turned away. "I've seen enough."

Liam Katani folded his arms. "So. Have. I."

I picked up a photo, male, young, his back shredded in the

first ones, then stages of healing with massive ropey keloid scars. "This you?"

He sighed. "Afraid so. I was brand new on the job. Compassionate like you guys. They were human once, right? Maybe we could help them. Maybe we could *cure* them. That's how I used to think back then. So I had her in the back of my car, transporting her to a psychiatric hospital. She'd had a massive dose of Haldol and it slowed her down and then she got . . . *worse*, is the only way I know to put it."

"Haldol?" I said. "You shouldn't be using that. That kind of med is outdated and dangerous for patients. It's invasive. There are better medications now and better ways to administer them and it's a damn shame that nursing homes and psychiatric units didn't get the memo. It can kill a patient in cognitive decline."

"I wasn't that lucky. This one was off the charts. Miriam Wilkerson. That ring a bell? Santa Clarita, California?"

"The teacher? Who was in what was thought to be a fatal car accident, then left the hospital morgue, and went to the classroom where her daughter was having band practice?"

"It was a fatal car accident, and she was a mirror twin, organs reversed, and she did regenerate. Yeah, that's her. Teacher of the year, five times in a row. Let me show you her daughter and some of her classmates. And yes, band practice, right?"

"Music again," Perry said.

"But the music did not calm her. It freaked her out. Like you said, Noah, triggering memories and not being able to handle the emotions."

More pictures. Victims not recognizable as human unless you already knew.

"Whoever it was that came back, that wasn't her. That is what I keep trying to tell you. The beloved teacher, mother, wife, who was such a talented ceramicist that she had just rented space for her own studio. Her work was known around the world. Tragic. Because what came back was not her. What came back was something *alien* and *off* and no longer human."

"But it was," Perry said. "She went back to her classroom. To her students. To her daughter. To the music. *So it was her.* I get that you want to call her not human, so you can compartmentalize and hunt her down and kill her. Because that's what you do, right? That's the part you are not saying out loud. You kill them. But she's human."

"Not a version of her you'd want on your front porch."

"Where is she now?"

"Captured. Euthanized. Cremated. Twice. Ashes returned to the family and they scattered them on Magic Mountain, God knows why."

"Did they know you killed her?"

"I don't tell the families that. I inform them of the sad death of the person they love and they cry and breathe a big sigh of relief because they have been terrified out of their minds."

"It's not just a physical regeneration going on, Katani. Erebus Lynch isn't just the regenerated body. There is something dark inside him."

"You're saying he's possessed, Noah?"

I nodded.

He frowned. "I believe you're right—that all resurrected mirror twins are possessed by spirits other than their own. It's one reason they are so violent and dangerous. But listen, Noah, this is not a possession as you know it. Think of skin-walkers, from Native American legends, a shapeshifting witch, malevolent. Dangerous as hell. Or the Loa, from Haitian Voodoo tradition. Intermediaries between humans and the creator. The Loa come only when they have a human body to access; they ride the body like a horse, they are in sync with the soul of the body, they come to indulge, with festivity, music, singing and dance. It's a sacred way to interact with powerful spirits, sometimes fallen spirits. And the fallen spirits have physical abilities, strength, the ability to withstand pain, and an angry Loa will go after the family.

"And honestly, Noah, from what I've seen, the extreme violence, the merciless killing, the literal tearing their victims apart—family members they loved all of their life. It would make sense that mirror twins attract something supernatural that ties the spiritual realm with the physical realm at the moment of physical regeneration—it may actually facilitate regeneration. That would make a certain sense. That could well be what happened to Erebus Lynch.

"And you, Perry—you're the shaman and you communicate with a spirit. You deal with dark influence. In Native American cultures it is called the Witchery Way. Initiation into the Witchery Way requires the murder of a close relative, especially a sibling, and once initiated into the Witchery Way one becomes pure evil. Again, the same thing. Going after family as soon as they regenerate. The pattern is consistent. They die, something dark, some kind of possession, some kind of witchery attaches, and they regenerate with that supernatural presence reborn just as they're reborn.

"At that point though they cannot be redeemed, they cannot be saved. Your exorcisms, your healing prayers, your baptism—none of this makes a difference. They have to be destroyed, or they will go after their families, and they will be merciless. Listen to me, I have seen it. I have seen the bodies torn to pieces. Bottom line—it doesn't matter what you call them or what possesses them, so long as you kill them and cremate them so that they can never return again. I have shown you the pictures. Do not waste your sympathy on those who are beyond help."

"No one is beyond help," Perry said. "This could be about timing. If you could be there at the moment of regeneration, perform an exorcism, protect them from any kind of dark entity that goes after them . . ." he shrugged. "Why not try?"

Katani rubbed his hand across his face. "*It won't matter*. Even if you prevent any kind of possession, the very process of regeneration brings them back as dangerous, violent and at that point they are not human."

"So you track them down and kill them," I said flatly.

"I save a lot of lives."

"But you track them down and kill them."

"Yes. Yes, I track them down and kill them."

"And, dangerous as they are, how do you do that?"

Katani leaned forward. "Do you really want to know?"

"How do you kill them?" I said.

"I hook them up to the winch on the back of the Tahoe. I go slow. I walk them to the nearest crematorium."

"And if they won't walk? If they can't walk? Or keep up?"

"Then I drag them."

The room got quiet, and Katani's face went dark.

Perry stood up and began to pace. "Brutal. Barbaric. Unnecessary."

"Wrong, Perry, *necessary*. Drugs don't work. Tie them up and put them in the back seat of your car and you won't get out of that car alive. They will tear you apart, and the car apart. Shoot them and they start regenerating."

I looked up at Chloe. "He has a database, doesn't he? Accessing medical records of mirror twins?"

She looked at Katani. "You do."

He nodded. "I do. And Erebus Lynch is one of them, a mirror twin regenerate. Not a zombie, because zombies by definition have lost their free will. And this dark, regenerated manifestation of a mirror twin who has the power to come back to life and follow their darkest impulses—they are not human; they have gone the Witchery Way. There is *no* hope for them. They have to be destroyed."

"I don't agree with that," Perry said. "And I don't like the brutality of your methods. They are still living beings and they should be given a chance to get free of the dark influences. They should be given compassion. I have known you since you were an eighteen-year-old college kid, Liam. What happened to you?"

"Miriam Wilkerson happened to me. Compassion almost got me killed. Keeping them around to come back yet again—it's too dangerous. You'd be risking the lives of innocents. People they loved before they died and resurrected. What do you think that mother in Santa Clarita would have chosen if she'd known she was going to come back and kill her own daughter?"

"I don't think she'd have chosen the winch," Perry said.

"She would have. To protect her child."

She'd have chosen whatever it took, I thought. To protect her daughter. Even if it was the winch.

NINETEEN

We had all gone very quiet, but Katani was gathering his materials together and didn't seem to notice. "Now. Next step. I can't get Lavinia Lynch to talk to me, and I've tried more than once to get her permission to exhume her husband's grave. She keeps telling me no."

"Why do you care?" I asked him.

"I have to document this. I need proof of the likelihood of regeneration. I'm going to head out when we're done here, catch her at home and in person, see if she'll finally talk to me about her husband and her son now Erebus is back for a second time and her whole family is in danger. She's got first-hand information and so far she's survived. I've never met another family member who did. Because *think*. She was married to one. She had a child with one. Twins. Mirror twins. One of them died. One of them always dies. The living twin makes sure of that."

I thought of Jesse, and the grief over his brother. "That's a ridiculous generalization."

"Again, documented. How many organs-reversed mirror twins have you run across in your work? Because I have a whole database of them. She lives close. I'm going to ring her doorbell and see if she'll talk."

"Why would she trust you?"

He gave me that smirk. "Maybe she'll like me in person. I have great hair and charm. You're frowning, Dr. Archer, why is that? Don't agree with the exhumation? Don't think I have great hair?"

"No, you have great hair. I've been thinking about exhumation too," I agreed. "It would be a good idea."

I was telling the truth. I believed in the supernatural, but that didn't make me any less of a scientist. I understood the logic of exhuming the grave, to see if Lynch's bones were still buried there—or if we truly were dealing with a living, breathing corpse.

But what I didn't get, and kept to myself, was why Lavee Lynch had already said no. Again, she was a step ahead of everyone else. Jesse was a situs inversus twin. Just like his dad. She must have been protecting Jesse. She knew Katani was trouble and she didn't want him anywhere near her son.

And I wondered. Had she told Jesse about his father regenerating? About how dangerous he was? Because Jesse had not told me about that and he would have. He'd have had a million questions. He'd wonder if he too would go rogue and be a danger to his family.

His mother was lying by omission and now he had kids on the way. And if there was a chance he could regenerate and come back as a danger to his family . . . Jesse should have been told. Given a choice to make up his own mind. Would he have even had children if he'd known they could be mirror twins, facing exactly what he was facing now?

"Has anybody informed Jesse of what could happen when he dies?" Katani asked. Looking straight at me, as if he'd read my thoughts.

"I'll be taking care of that. Do not put him in your data file."

"Too late," Katani said.

"With any luck he'll outlive you."

"I don't call that luck. And I'll be out exhuming the grave of Erebus Lynch at ten thirty a.m. tomorrow whether Mrs. Lynch says yes or no. Join me if you want. That way we can prove once and for all exactly what Erebus Lynch is, and I can take care of him and make sure he never bothers anyone ever again."

Perry looked at Chloe. She didn't say anything. And by that I knew she was all in. Academics can't be stopped by mere laws.

Exhuming graves did not disturb me. The look in Agent Liam Katani's eyes did. This was a hatred that ran deep.

"And I'm sorry, Chloe, truly I am. But I'll be taking that frozen hand, and the cigar butts, and the results of your tests."

She turned and glared at him. “Consider yourself told no.”

“Look outside.”

Three more Tahoes in the parking lot. Men and women in uniform milling around.

“You want me to ask my colleagues to come in? They make a hell of a mess when they do. Just hand the stuff over.”

Chloe refused. So we did it the hard way. Standing in our own offices and our own lab, while law enforcement came in, took everything they wanted, and gutted our lab.

TWENTY

Chloe paced the lab in a fury, tears running down her cheeks. Perry caught her hand as she walked by him, and he pulled her close. She sat on the edge of his chair, and he put his arm around her.

"What happened to him, Perry? I've known Liam since he was seventeen. He was a great kid. A *nice* kid. Brilliant and shy and an absolute sweetheart."

"I remember," Perry said. He glanced over at me. "He really was."

Chloe bit her lip. "I trusted him."

I turned away from the window. "And I trusted you."

She turned to face me. Perry kept hold of her hand.

I folded my arms, leaning back against the wall. "We maintain strict confidentiality with our patients, with the people we help. They have need of privacy, and it's up to us to keep their sensitive information secure. Do you see what you've facilitated, Chloe? Katani's database he uses to target mirror twins and winch them out of the world. I mean, for fuck's sake, have you ever heard of HIPAA? Don't you protect your own research? From poaching academics, and big pharma, and the government who would be happy to use it for their own agenda?"

Chloe stood up and paced across the room. "Do you think I gave him access to our files?"

"Sounds like you did."

"No, Noah. Of course I didn't. I did discuss Erebus Lynch with him and gave him the 'dead but not dead' results from the severed hand and the cigar butts. I didn't give names . . . but I must have given him enough information so that he didn't need names, not with the database he's collected. Still. The paper files those guys took? It was just research information I had to hand. Anything really critical is in an encrypted file on my server. Paper is just a failsafe for the computerized data, and I'm phasing it out, so he got random files that won't interest him much. He did get the severed hand and the cigar butts, yes, and it's annoying as hell, but I've already done the testing and I have the results. All that was just theater, Noah, to intimidate, a power play."

"You still crossed a line, Chloe."

"Yes. I did. I gave him enough details to identify Jesse Lynch. And worse still, he'll be tracking Lola and her babies."

"And there's nothing we can do?"

She folded her arms. "I didn't say that. As my system of work is vulnerable to someone like Liam who has worked with me closely and knows me well, so too is his."

"What are you going to do?" Perry asked.

"The question," Chloe said, "is what are *we* going to do? Let's take a vote."

"What are our options?"

"Defcon Three, we access all his data. Defcon Two, we access his material and compromise it so that it quickly becomes useless to him. Defcon One, we erase the databases he keeps, which means none of us have access and mirror twins are at less risk. But keep in mind, because thanks to Palantir Tech, which our government has gone wild with, he will always be able to data mine all government databases and get the information again. But it will slow him down."

"Defcon Three for now gets my vote," I said. "But whatever choice we make, we remove Jesse and Lola and her babies from both of the databases. I know that Liam knows. I know he can put them back in. But we must do our best to keep them out of there to protect them from anyone else."

"Defcon Three. Keep him rolling and keep an eye on what he is up to." She looked over at Perry.

"Defcon One," Perry said. "Because it provides the best level of protection to mirror twins in that database. Living or dead."

I looked back out the window, making sure Katani and his people were gone. "Let's start with Defcon Three and sit with this a while, and take another vote in a few days."

"I'm sorry, Noah," Chloe said.

"I know."

TWENTY-ONE

The call for help came through just minutes after Agent Katani left. Lola, in a WhatsApp video call. I could see the echoes of horror in her face, hear the frantic high pitch of her voice, see the healing red streak where Erebus Lynch had scratched her face.

She was sprawled on the floor, back to the wall. "*He's here.* Jesse went after him. We—"

"Where are you, Lola?"

"Manchester Music Hall, rehearsing *Bad Dad Tango*. It's—"

"I know where it is—I'm right across the street. Stay where you are and stay safe, I'm on my way."

"Oh, God. *Hurry.*"

"Fast as I can."

Perry was up and on his feet. He looked at Chloe.

"I'll be right behind you. I'll need my kit." She was the science part of the team.

I was three strides ahead of Perry. "Car or run?" he said. Because it was that close. Five tenths of a mile.

"Car," I said.

We were there in three minutes.

They were waiting for us when we burst through the door. Actors, musicians, stagehands, clustered around Lola, stepping around equipment, a small, intimate venue, a stage, a woman who said *he's here.*

Lola was on the floor, sitting up, back to the wall, eyes wide. "I'm OK, I'm OK. Jesse went after him that way down the hall. Please, please don't let him hurt my husband."

I exchanged looks with Perry. He headed down the hall, and I crouched down next to Lola, who was not OK.

A lot of buzz and conversation behind me. I looked at the

woman who had led me to Lola. She was older than the rest. In charge.

"Can you get me a blanket?"

"On it."

Lola's breathing was erratic and her left pupil was blown, the right a narrow pinpoint.

"Looks like you hit your head," I said gently, in that confident voice a patient needs to hear.

"No, no, I just fell, I got scared and was backing up and—"

The woman brought me the blanket, and I tucked it around Lola's shoulders.

"You've called 911?"

"Yes. And I have the attack on video. That man was . . . a monster. It's on my phone."

"You are awesome. Let me see to Lola, but will you text me a copy?" I gave her my number. "Any minute now we'll have cops and paramedics. The paramedics will get here first; there's a firehouse right on Merino, they have a great crew—" I heard the sirens. They were right behind me.

I smiled down at Lola. "OK if I look after you here?"

She nodded.

"I'm going to ease you down—"

"No, no, I'm sick to my stomach. I have to sit up or I'll puke."

"Well, we can't have that. Were you feeling sick before you fell?"

"Yes, I—they may call it morning sickness but it lasts all day. You've got to go—"

"Perry is on his way to Jesse. I'm here for you. You and your babies."

"Yes—look after my babies. But really, I'm OK."

"That's good news. Can you tell me where you are?"

Nothing.

"Can you tell me your name?"

The look of confusion that passed over her face made me worry. She gave me that smile patients give me when they are not really *not* OK; when they're scared and don't want to admit it. Her teeth were chattering, breathing shallow and rapid. I touched the carotid artery gently where the pulse was jumping. She was going right into shock.

The doors behind me opened, and I could hear murmurs and the rustle of people stepping back and out of the way. I glanced over my shoulder, saw the pulse of the emergency lights from the truck, two guys coming through the door, two more behind them. The cavalry was here.

"Hey, Sid," I said, recognizing the paramedic.

"Dr. Archer? What's going on?" He was as glad to see me as I was to see him.

"Sid, meet my patient, Lola Strickler. She's in the early weeks of pregnancy, she's had a shock and a fall, she's dehydrated and concussed. Can you get an IV started up?"

"I'm on it." He gave her a look then back to me. "Shock?"

"Let's get ahead of that. Lola, this is Sid, and he's pretty great. He's going to start an IV and give you and those babies some fluids, OK? Have you been able to keep any food down the last two or three days?"

"No," she said softly.

I told him where I wanted her to be admitted. "Who's your OBGYN, Lola?"

"I don't . . . Oh God, I can't remember. Jesse knows. I need Jesse."

"I'll get him for you. Sid's going to get you to the ER—"

"No, I don't want to go to the hospital . . ."

I squeezed her hand. "Nobody ever does."

"You're a brain surgeon. I don't want brain surgery."

Sid and I exchanged looks. She wasn't tracking.

"Lola, most head injuries resolve on their own. I'm just going to have you monitored, checked out, and I will see you back at the hospital as soon as I can."

"And you'll get Jesse?"

"I'll get Jesse. I'll stay with you until—"

"No. No. Go get Jesse."

"Hey, Lola," Sid said. "Don't mind me, I'm just looking for a vein. Is Jesse your husband?"

She nodded. Winced. I ran my fingers gently over the back

of her skull, found the swelling. She'd gone down hard and I'd need to run some tests.

"Lola, I'm going to step away here, let Sid take over. I'll call the hospital and get everything set up for you, is that OK? Lola, that OK?"

She closed her eyes. "Sleepy," she said.

Not good. She lost consciousness before they had her on the gurney.

TWENTY-TWO

It was either a standoff or a moment of calm. Maybe a bit of both. Jesse, disheveled, angry, looking just as shocked as Lola. Perry standing calmly, eyes trained on the man, the creature. The regeneration of Erebus Lynch.

He looked human and yet other. In the time since Lola had taken the video, he had gone downhill fast and had the look of a man in stage-four dementia. His left hand, which had been severed by his wife with a chainsaw, was oversized, pulsing, and looked oddly dangerous. He was staring at Perry, whose hands were at his sides, whose voice was gentle and strong with the gentle gravitas I recognized from the exorcisms he had done. Like one man talking another off a ledge. Or banishing a dark entity back to God. "No one is going to hurt you. You're safe here. It's OK to be confused." The cadence of his words was hypnotic.

Jesse kept his gaze on his father. "Lola—"

"Is going to be OK," I said.

Erebus Lynch was agitated, uncertain, rocking back and forth, a tall man, painfully thin with emaciation, bones and very little flesh but with the wiry tensile strength of a cat. I had seen this in so many patients, the way he stood, like a man who knew he was off balance, the way his eyes went from dull to fierce. The dystonia in his facial muscles that caused the lack of expression on his face. He opened his mouth and screamed and yet there was no sound.

"Why does he do that?" Jesse said. He was holding a baseball bat, gripping it tight.

"He's trying to talk," I said. "But he can't. The vocal cords are compromised. He probably can't swallow either. If he tries to eat or drink, he'll choke."

Erebus Lynch reminded me of patients I had, ones with dementia, Parkinson's, severe brain damage from TBIs. I saw confusion, and that borderline territory of rage and pain, the disoriented fear of a man in cognitive stress, who lived in a world that no longer made sense. Most of my patients were struggling *not* to hurt anyone that they loved. But not Lynch. I had seen that look before, in the eyes of possessed patients who were long gone into the darkness. Who embraced it.

Perry saw it too. "Listen, Noah, I'm going to give this a shot, here and now. It may be our only chance to confront him and help him find a way out."

I nodded. Looked at Jesse. "Hang on to that baseball bat, Jesse, but step back."

Perry didn't take his eyes off Lynch.

"*I call to Joan of Arc, I call to Mary Mother of God, I call to St. Michael the Archangel, to protect Erebus Lynch from the darkness within, to give him the courage to be valiant. I ask that you shield and save anything of Erebus Lynch that has not been lost, to intercede and cast out the dark spirit who seeks the ruin of his soul, and send it back to God.*"

For Erebus Lynch the struggle was escalating with a speed I had not seen before, and it showed in the lines in his face, the tension in his shoulders, and the way his hands twitched, and squeezed into fists, a pulse that was building inside him. Say the wrong thing, make the wrong move, and he would erupt.

"Are you really my father?" Jesse said softly.

Erebus looked at him. Groaned. Choked.

"I can help you," Perry said. Holding out a hand.

Erebus Lynch looked at me. Curious, wary, and then I was dismissed. He opened his mouth wide. He began to sing. A raspy, thin, reedy and rusty voice. "Moon River". He sang the first verse, staring hard at Jesse.

"You sang that when you killed Frankie," Jessie said. "You don't deserve help." And Jesse, a look of fury on his face, started swinging the baseball bat.

Erebus took a hard blow on his shoulder and his hip, tilted his head, roared at his son, then lunged. Jesse went sideways, but was fast on his feet, and the blood was flying.

That's when the cops arrived.

Only they were going after Jesse. And while they wrestled him to the ground, Erebus Lynch ran.

TWENTY-THREE

The woman who filmed the video of Erebus Lynch going after Lola was the hero of the day. Two officers, then four more arrived, but the video was compelling. In the clip, Lola was playing "Moon River" on her saxophone, so deep in concentration she was not aware of Erebus Lynch standing right behind her on the stage until the shouting started, cast members warning her to run. By then it was too late. He grabbed her by the shoulders, shaking her, then lifted her up and slammed her into the floor.

And there was Jesse, moving fast, heading up to the stage and grabbing his father, who took off running. We saw Jesse bending down to Lola, wrapping his arms around her, the look of horror as she saw over her shoulder that Erebus Lynch was back.

Jesse kissed her, and took off after his father, who ran.

"Do you know who he is?" This question was from the officer in charge, young, female, an air of professional competence. She was looking at Jesse.

"He looks shockingly like my father, who died when I was fourteen. Unless you're telling me my dad came back from the dead, I have no idea who he is. But whoever he is, he's been hanging out around my house, and I think he's stalking my wife. You saw it on the video, the way he attacked her. It looks like he's the same man who attacked her at our house before."

Masterful. Nothing like the truth.

She nodded. "This is going to be turned over to our Detective unit. I'm going to give you a copy of the police report, the number is right there at the top, the detectives should get in touch, but they're busy down there so, if you don't hear back pretty quick, go on and give them a call."

"I need to go to the hospital and see my wife."

"Understood, sir. In the meantime, we'll be rounding up the

paperwork on her injuries, and yours, and I'm heading over to the hospital to interview her."

"Hold off until tomorrow, if you would," I interjected. "I'm her doctor and she's in no condition right now to be interviewed."

"I'll stop in tomorrow afternoon then." She handed Jesse a copy of the report and she and the two other officers filed out.

Jesse gave me a look. "So now you've met my father too," he said softly. "And it just keeps getting worse and worse, which it always does with my dad. I should maybe call my mother and tell her to watch out, in case he comes after her. She's probably next on his list, and I better tell Ray." He shook his head. "He was so strong, man, and angry as hell; it's like wrestling with the Incredible Hulk. I don't get how he can be here. I always thought he died."

"Jesse, your mom knows how dangerous your father is. She's known a long time. And your father did die. Twice. This has happened before."

"What? Are you saying he came back *before*?"

"Yes. You were nineteen, in college."

He puzzled over that. "I remember. I told her I thought I saw his gold Cadillac, but I never . . . Look, I can't think about this right now."

He staggered forward and I took his arm.

"Sorry, sorry, I just flashed on that moment when he picked Lola up and slammed her down to the ground. You sure she's OK—the babies?"

"She hit her head and she's on her way to the hospital, probably in the ER by now. I'll take you to her, we'll go together, she needs you. She's hurt, Jesse, but I'm as optimistic as I can be that she'll be home with you soon."

Jesse began hyperventilating, sweating and gasping for breath. Perry and I grabbed him before he went down and settled him onto an old chair next to a stack of crates. He looked up at me, face white, shut his eyes very tight, groaned and bent forward.

"Tell me what you're feeling right now." I held his wrist, tracking his pulse.

"Like I'm having a heart attack." His voice was tight.

"It's a panic attack, Jesse, not your first, so you know it's going to pass. Just take steady breaths, yes, just like that. Lola is OK, I'm right here, your father is gone."

"I still don't want any meds."

The only thing I could prescribe were benzos or SSRIs and none of them would do him any good.

"I think a panic attack is a reasonable response to your dead father coming after your wife. I don't think medicating you out of common sense is a good idea."

Jesse looked up at me, then laughed. He started to get up but I shook my head.

"Take a minute," I told him, hand on his shoulder. "Make sure you're steady on your feet."

It took a while. But his color flooded back and his breathing steadied.

"I didn't pass out this time," Jesse said.

"Progress."

"I need to get Lola's sax. She'll go crazy if I don't."

"We'll grab it on our way out."

Perry gave me a look. "Chloe is out front doing her thing. I'll talk to everybody here and we'll regroup later. Right now—go be a doctor."

I nodded. It's what I do.

On the way to the hospital, Jesse wanted every last detail about Lola, and I told him everything I knew in a way that was honest without going to catastrophic places.

"And now I have a question for you, Jesse."

He glanced over at me.

"Why was Lola playing 'Moon River'?"

Jesse leaned back in the seat and looked away. "Some of the music in *Bad Dad Tango* is . . . personal to me. You know about Frankie. And Dad always sang that one. He would play it too, you know, Audrey Hepburn singing, and grab my mother and me, dance us around the room. But Mom always cried because we all knew what that song meant. Dad didn't want to be there, at home with us. He wanted to be free, and off in the world."

"Well. You could say he got what he wanted."

Jesse sputtered then laughed. "You're as bad as Ray. You think he's here . . . that I called him back, with my play? The music?"

"Maybe."

"I thought we'd like . . . do some kind of exorcism and he'd be gone. But Perry did one, and—"

"It's not going to work if it goes against his will. They have to want to come back. They have to want to let go of the darkness."

'I thought I saw something," Jesse said. "Like he wavered. But maybe not."

"Your father is pretty far gone, mentally and physically. He's not really in any condition to go through an exorcism, but that's how it works most of the time. People are often in really bad shape, and we don't have any choice because they're only going to get worse."

"What the hell does that mean? What kind of condition could he be in? Why would we worry about him getting worse? I mean we . . . we buried him when I was fourteen. Did my mother lie? Was the funeral a sham and he didn't die back then?"

"Yes and no. Your mother lied but he definitively died. Then he came back—and now he's done the same again."

"So he's a ghost?"

"I thought so at first. But the evidence suggests he's regenerating. Coming back to life, but in a bad mental state. And his might not be the only spirit inside his body."

Jesse didn't take it well. He shut his eyes tight. "I'm having trouble wrapping my mind around this."

"I am too, and he's not my father."

"Yeah but . . . is he living or dead? Or does that matter?"

"He's kind of both. And yes, it matters."

"So you don't think an exorcism will work?"

I thought about it. "I think it was worth a shot. Because I think something dark has attached to your father. Maybe years before he died. Only Perry will know if we should try this again. Because every time we do it and fail? Your father gets that much more dangerous. And God knows he's dangerous enough as he is. It might not be worth the risk."

"To him or the rest of us?" Jesse asked.

"The rest of us."

He nodded. He had clearly come to that conclusion already.

"There's more, Jesse."

"Like what?"

"Want to know now? I know you're upset about Lola."

"Yes, I want to know now."

So I filled him in. On everything. Agent Katani, his hunting of regenerates, that he was after Jesse's father. That he had it in his database that Jesse himself was a situs inversus mirror twin.

"That means . . ."

It didn't take him long to figure it out.

"So I could come back, like my dad? But not really human anymore? I could go after Lola and our babies some day?"

"That's a lot of ifs, Jesse. But yes, I won't lie to you, it's in the realm of possibility. But you can set things up so that can't happen. You're not helpless here; this can be managed. People manage health issues every day."

"*Health issues*?" He gave a hard laugh. "And let me get this straight. My mother knew and didn't tell me? She let Lola and me get pregnant, not knowing?"

I nodded.

"How long have *you* known?"

"Since this morning—and before I could tell you, Lola called."

"Thank you. For telling me. The only thing that matters is Lola and our babies. And I'll have a decision to make."

I looked up at him. "Which is?"

"Which one to kill first—my mother or my father. How did that Agent Katani find out about my father? Did my mother tell him?"

"Your mother? No. She won't give him the time of day. He tracks situs inversus mirror twins, and when Chloe contacted him, he was already hot on the trail. He's a Fed; he's got access to the Palantir deep state system the government has been funding for years now; it cross-references all major databases, and he can find out everything he wants to know. On all of us."

"I get it. Remember when HIPAA was a big deal?"

"The good old days."

"And this . . . this is something you can help us with? Me and Lola. Something you and Perry can handle?"

"We'll do our best."

I gave him my most confident smile, and he leaned his head back, closed his eyes tight, and sighed.

He'd bought it.

Medical training instilled the automatic facade of all-knowing confidence, which didn't do anybody any good. But it was hard for me to break the habit. Dr. Noah Archer, neurologist extraordinaire, healing the living . . . and the dead.

Perry and I would just have to figure out how.

TWENTY-FOUR

My pager went off as we pulled into the hospital parking garage. Questions about tests for Lola and two other patients in crisis by the time I got to the ER.

"Are they paging you about my wife?"

"They are. Confirming the tests I ordered, so they're getting to her fast. She's stabilized and conscious and that's very good."

"Is it always like this for you?"

"Pretty much."

Lola did not have a brain bleed, but she was severely dehydrated from morning sickness and vomiting, and she had a concussion. I was keeping her in overnight, coordinating with her obstetrician who knew she fell but not why. She hadn't been interested enough to ask. Lola wanted to keep the details confidential and I didn't blame her. Your average doctor does not deal well with things like this.

When I left, Jesse was dozing in a chair beside her bed, holding her hand while she slept. She could go home in the morning; she'd need to take it easy, and as we always tell them . . . try not to fall again for at least a year. Lola promised that the saxophone would be her only contact sport.

I wasn't going to make it home anytime soon. I had two other patients in crisis, and a family who wanted to discuss taking one of them off life support. Which, in my opinion, would be the right call.

My brain tumor nursing-student patient was doing well, no malignancy, and his children had come to cheer him on. My TBI patient, who had lost the reins and one stirrup on a runaway horse and been dragged halfway across a paddock, who had been fighting so hard for her life in a battle she was unlikely to win, began spiraling and slid into a deep coma, and before her family had to make a final decision, it was over.

That kind of thing happened a lot in my line of work. Considering the extent of her injuries, death would have been my choice, but I did not think it was hers; she'd been fighting hard. Her last conscious thoughts were for her horse who had been spooked but was already safe and loved in the barn. So that was something.

I checked in on my two other surgery patients. Both doing damn well.

I stopped in my office and caught up on paperwork, too restless to go home, until the fatigue hit, and I shut down my computer and headed out.

I didn't make it. My pager went off. Code grey—a violent or aggressive person, combative, possible security intervention needed.

I knew what that meant. Jesse's mother was here.

TWENTY-FIVE

Ray was urbane, in a suit and tie, deeply etched lines in his face, sunken hooded eyes, and clearly worried about Lola. His gravitas and charisma meant he had the attention of every single person in the room, including me.

He went straight to Lola and took her hand. "Pretty Lola. I am so sorry you got hurt. There is nothing your mother and I won't do for you and those babies."

"*Jesse's* mother," Lola said, voice curt.

Ray turned away. "Jesse?"

Jesse was up on his feet and they had a quick, hard, man hug, and I knew that Ray meant the world to Jesse. Ray had been his official father since the age of fourteen, but he'd been around earlier, I'd bet, long before the death of Erebus Lynch, a hero to a boy who was being suffocated by a father who disapproved of him and kept a heavy hand on his shoulder. I understood Lola, but I was on Team Ray. Maybe it was a guy thing.

Lavee Lynch wasn't in the room anymore. Jesse had asked her to leave, and I could hear her heels clicking down the hallway, voice high pitched and angry. "I will see Dr. Archer *right now.*"

She sounded hurt and unsure, but she had brought it on herself.

I headed out into the corridor and she came toward me, so single-minded she didn't notice the two security guards bearing down on her from the other end of the hall.

"Mrs. Lynch. Will you come with me to my office for a fifteen-minute consult?"

"Yes, thank you."

Then the two security guards behind her looked at me and I nodded. "Follow me, it's this way."

"But what about Lola?" Lavee demanded.

"Lola is doing OK; she'll be going home with Jesse tomorrow morning."

"Jesse won't let me see her."

"He's upset. So is Lola. Let them have their space."

She looked over her shoulders at the security guards, face tight, but she was as smart as she was pissed off. "Fine. I would appreciate that fifteen-minute consult. Thank you, Dr. Archer."

"Right this way."

I waved the security guards off.

TWENTY-SIX

Lavee Lynch perched on the edge of the chair across from my desk and gave me a wary look. "I love my son, his wife is having twins, and there is nothing I won't do to protect them."

"Except tell them the truth."

"Which, as Jesse told me before he kicked me out of Lola's hospital room, you did for me. How *could* you? You didn't just tell Jesse; you told Lola too. Not just about Jesse's father, but about his own genetic risk. And now he thinks he might be a danger to his wife and children, and he is so upset at the thought that I know . . . *I know*—"

I waited.

"I know he would not have chosen to have children. To pass this on. To be a danger to them when he dies. He's worried he will resurrect."

"He should be worried. And it should have been his choice—*and Lola's*—whether or not to bring children at risk in the world. Their choice and not yours, and you forced their hand because . . ." I took a breath.

I had to stop there. I had seen this play out, with patients and their families, known up close and personal the misery that came with family secrets. I'm sure Lavee Lynch thought she was protecting her son, even though she was making things worse because you can't deal with things you don't know.

"I should have told them," she conceded. "But I didn't want them to live under this kind of shadow. I've spent my life protecting Jesse from this kind of thing. I understand he feels betrayed right now, even though I did it for his sake. And maybe . . . maybe I did betray him by not telling him the truth."

I felt sorry for Lavee, though I appreciated her hard-won effort not to cry. I had seen this before, more times than I could count. Families keeping their genetic diseases secret. Pretending it was a kindness, leaving their children—often their adult children—bewildered by symptoms, spending years trying to figure out if something was wrong and what it might be. Robbing them of the chance to plan their life factoring the illness in, and standing silently by, withholding information even when they found themselves back to the wall again and again with symptoms as crushing as they were inexplicable. Symptoms their families recognized and yet said not a word.

Time and again, my patients came to me saying their illnesses could *not* be the one that kept popping up on Google each time they searched desperately for an answer, because *if it ran in the family they would have been told.*

She took a breath. “OK. I admit I was wrong. I didn’t want to face the fallout of Jesse knowing. Ray isn’t happy with me about this. But I just . . . wanted it all to be OK somehow. I wanted Erebus and his dark presence to go away and stay away, and I wanted to pretend it wasn’t real. I wish sometimes I didn’t know. That I could be free of worrying about this. Erebus and I have been apart for years and yet still he seems to control my life. I didn’t want him controlling Jesse’s life.”

I got up and shut the office door. The last thing we needed was to be overheard.

I nodded. Settled back in my chair. “I get that. And Jesse has the right to a life he chooses, to find his place in the world. So does Lola, and so do their twins. But keeping this secret is not loving them.”

“Are you saying Jesse should not have children?”

“I’m saying it’s a decision he and Lola needed to make themselves and they deserved to know the risks. Lola is now pregnant with twin girls. There’s a strong possibility they’ll be mirror twins like Jesse and Frankie.”

“I always meant to tell him. I just kept putting it off.” She folded her hands neatly in her lap. “I don’t think Jesse will ever forgive me.”

“My advice is to give him time and space to process this. Lola and Jesse have been bewildered to see his *dead* father inexplicably show up at their condo, follow them in his car. They were terrified and worried and even so they still had no idea how dangerous he is. Don't you think Jesse should have known, for his own good?"

She looked away.

"It was a stroke of random luck that Lola wasn't hurt really badly and didn't lose those babies. If she'd fractured her skull, had a brain bleed, slid into coma? Imagine the kind of conversation we'd be having now. Have you seen the video?" I took my phone out, brought the video up, and tried to hand it to her.

"No, no, I can't—"

That's when the tears started and I didn't much care.

She took the phone. Watched the video, and sobbed, then gasped. "I kept hoping somehow they would never have to know."

I took the phone out of her hands.

"Erebus has always been dangerous to Jesse," Lavee said quietly. "I've protected him since he was born. Him and Frankie. You just get used to staying quiet and keeping watch. Erebus wasn't a bad man. He loved Jesse fiercely, and the only reason he stayed in this town was because of him. You have to understand that so much of what he did that turned out bad—it was love for Jesse and the yearning for a different life."

"And Frankie?"

She put her face in her hands. "I didn't know he'd killed Frankie. Not until you told me about Jesse's dream."

"Why you let a guy like that off the hook, I'll never understand. Your husband just didn't want to be a father. He didn't want the responsibility of fatherhood. But he didn't have the courage to cut you and your sons loose, so you could have a better life without his crap. He wanted it both ways. You got to make *your* own decisions. When to stay and when to go, and when to kill your husband with a chainsaw. Jesse should get to make his own decisions too."

She winced.

"Look, we all do it. Lies of omission. But when you get found out, you can lose the people you're trying to protect. The best thing you can do is trust Jesse to handle things, let him live his life his way. But whatever else you know . . . don't keep Jesse in the dark. It's my experience that people have more trouble being lied to by people they love and trust than they do with whatever you're trying to keep from them."

She jerked her head up. "So easy for you to judge, but I was raised in a world where everything important was never actually discussed. And even when you try to tell them the truth, they don't really hear you, they don't understand. Most people say, 'just get a divorce'. I grew up in an era when mothers were blamed for being cold when they had a child who was on the spectrum. Where women were told they attracted and secretly wanted bad men, and that they subconsciously wanted to marry them. That somehow, some way, I got something out of our relationship, and that's why I married him. Their arrogant and blatantly idiotic and disrespectful assumptions on why I stayed. In other words—"

"It was all your fault. And you were held accountable for everything that went wrong, and held to impossible standards, and if your husband taught your son the fine art of belching, he was exalted into golden fatherhood and the world would applaud, while you did the heavy lifting. Things actually haven't changed that much."

She frowned at me. "At least you get it."

"I understand you had it hard. I understand you've spent years of your life trying to keep Jesse safe, especially after losing Frankie. It doesn't give you the right to lie by omission, lies that will cause nothing but trouble for the son you say you love. I know this because I once made the same mistake."

"Did that person . . . did they ever forgive you?"

"Yeah. I was lucky. But you don't want to put yourself at the mercy of luck. That's no kind of love if you ask me, and I had to learn that the hard way."

"Try to understand what this was like. My husband was a mirror twin. The other one died. That's what he called Frankie. *The other one.* Jesse's big brother, and as hard as that sounds, that was the way Erebus had of avoiding grief. But it was there, believe me, like it was there for me and for Jesse when Frankie died. That does not go away."

"And Erebus?"

"I honestly did not think I would survive after Frankie died. Married to the man I now know killed him, my sweet beautiful little Frankie. I think I always suspected, deep down, even if I never admitted it to myself. And I think he knew I suspected, and he was always waiting, I think, for me to do something. To take Jesse away—the one son he truly loved. Superficially glib, philosophical, and he didn't bury those feelings, oh no, they morphed into a terror of losing Jesse. And he became the king of codependent parents. He wasn't going to be overprotective. No. He would teach Jesse to be a man in the world and make sure Jesse had a perfect life, defined by what Erebus thought was a perfect life."

"Welcome to hell, Jesse."

"Exactly. I was so oblivious back then. I didn't know that my husband's grief went very dark. It wasn't grief over Frankie, over the unforgiveable crime he'd committed in a rush of temper. It was grief over not getting the life he felt entitled to. And Jesse? So much better than his father could ever be? He'll lose Lola, now she knows the truth. And he loves her so much. But she'll leave him. Lola will divorce him. He won't get to raise his babies. They'll live under a shadow; it will weigh down their lives, just like it has weighed down mine. It will destroy their marriage and—"

"It's a lot of work, trying to manage someone else's life," I interrupted. "Aren't you tired? Doesn't it wear you out?"

She looked away, thinking. "I never thought of it that way before. But the answer is yes. I am tired. More tired than you can possibly imagine. But all I can see is that you've just put my son in danger—and not just of losing his beloved wife. If word gets out that Jesse is a mirror twin himself, Agent Katani will take him down. Brutally."

"Agent Katani already knows. He's seen Jesse's medical records. He tracks mirror twins."

"That's not legal."

I made an effort to gentle my voice. "Yeah, legal went out the window a long time ago. He works for the Department of Defense and he has access to anything he wants if he can make their computers work."

She looked away. “You know what the worst thing about this is? I really did my best. I gave it everything I had, and I still messed it up.”

“Yeah, that’s actually just the definition of parenthood.”

I saw the moment of shock and then she actually laughed. “Maybe it’s time to lighten up and realize that in a world where your evil dead husband can actually come back to life, you might as well get on with the good stuff. Because the world is too fucked up to fix.”

“Words to live by.”

TWENTY-SEVEN

I made it home quickly, the streets full of Saturday-night bustle. But when I finally pulled up in my driveway, everything hit me at once. And it happened again, like it does sometimes. I could not summon the will to get out of the car.

I sat in the driveway, turned off the engine, and waited it out, my personal manifestation of system overload.

The front door opened, and late as it was the boys were still up. I saw the warmth and glow of the lights inside, my sons Vaughn and Marcus, rumpled jeans, tee shirts, and sock footed. As close as brothers could be.

"Go tell Mama that Daddy needs help," Vaughn told Marcus, who turned and ran back into the house. My children know me way too well.

Vaughn ran to the car, Tash barking and running ahead of him, scrabbling with her paws on the door of the car. Vaughn said, "Down, Tashie," opened the car door, and gave me his hand. "One of those days at work?"

I nodded.

I took his hand and then I was OK, and part of me didn't like it—I did not want my boys to have to take care of me—but the other part of me was grateful and relieved. And proud. Of him. Of me, not so much. It messed with my superhero status.

I found Moira in the kitchen, on her laptop, doing the endless work of a dedicated teacher. I smelled the pasta sauce cooling on the stovetop.

"Did you cook?" I asked.

"He says in a tone of shock." She shook her head. "Marcus."

"Oh good."

"Yeah, his pasta sauce is better than—" She gave me a look, stood up and wrapped me in her arms. "Yeah, Vaughn told me you had something of a day."

I looked over her shoulder at the kitchen mess, the cat curled up like a meatloaf in front of the stove, and it didn't register. What I saw was my own father. What would it be like if he came back one day and sang me a song? Would I be afraid of him, if he did?

Late that night when Moira and I curled up in bed, I told her everything. Including about my dad.

"What song do you think he'd have sung to you?"

"I have no idea, and it's driving me crazy. Probably the theme song of the old *Rawhide* show."

She smiled. "Call your mother tomorrow and ask her, she'll know."

"Good idea. And now—"

"Oh god, Noah, I love you but I am so damn tired."

"Give me ten minutes. Then if you want me to stop, no harm no foul."

"Do I get a back massage?"

"That's where I'll *start*."

I gave her my naughty smile, which I was convinced she would not be able to resist.

"Think you can get me interested in ten minutes?"

It only took five.

TWENTY-EIGHT

It was a pretty place, on a sunny afternoon, the green cemetery where Erebus Lynch had been buried. Twice.

There were horses in an adjoining field, and Perry and I walked the rise and fall of the gentle sloping hillside, the dark green bluegrass pasture, under sky-high black walnut trees. It seemed like a good place to wind up at the end of your life.

Lavinia Lynch was waiting for us. Five of us now, including Perry, Chloe, Katani, and me.

"This isn't legal," she said.

"We have your son's permission," Katani said. "And the permission of the owners. So yeah, it's legal."

"You told Jesse about this?" She looked shocked. "I will take you to court over this."

Katani nodded. "Do what you need to do." He hefted his shovel. "Are you sure you want to stay?"

"Don't patronize me. Ray and I dug this grave a second time when I killed Erebus in the garage."

"How?" Katani said.

"Chainsaw."

I could see him suppressing a smile. "That'll do it. And then you brought him back here?"

"Wrapped in a rug, but dead. The best place to hide a body is putting it back where it was."

"If you had cremated him, he wouldn't have come back."

"Good to know." She glanced over at me and I tried not to smile.

"Did you leave it like this? Churned up?"

"No. Are you saying Erebus dug his way out?"

"That's what I'm saying. Weird as it sounds."

"Weird is when your dead husband is driving a gold Cadillac and leaving cigar butts in the street outside your house. After that . . ." She waved a hand.

Katani gave her a look. “I do understand. Maybe more than anyone else you’ll ever meet. I also know he is going to target you again, you and Jesse and anyone in your family he loved and didn’t love.”

“I know this. I have lived with this. The only person who ever believed me was Ray. How is it *you* know this?”

“I have dealt with creatures like your husband before.”

“I have to admit, I like your approach. No obligation to pretend you felt compassion. He’s a creature to be dealt with. I’ve always looked at him that way, but never admitted it.”

“Set yourself free, Mrs. Lynch.”

“What will you do with him if you catch him?”

He tilted his head to one side, considering.

“This man is a danger to me. I really want to know.”

He gave Chloe a quick look and she nodded. “Same thing I did to the last one. I will . . . manage his death. In such a way that he does not come back.”

“Brutal,” Lavee said.

We were all thinking about the chainsaw, but nobody brought it up.

Katani cocked his head to one side. “You think he wants to come back to life in the state that he’s in? Confused, barely functioning. Then dying yet again? To me, leaving him to suffer that way would be brutal.”

“You work for the government,” Perry said. “They sanction this?”

Katani gave him a lopsided smile. “As you might have noticed, the government has a lot of leeway these days.”

“This is a living being.”

Katani looked away. Then back again. “These are creatures of regeneration. You think it has a soul?”

“He started with one. So yes, I think he does.”

“When doctors regenerate body parts, using stem cells or even using organ transplants—do you think these body parts have a soul?”

I’d always wondered that myself, and I leaned toward yes. It was why I’d never consider an organ transplant. I don’t want that kind of intimacy with the soul of a stranger. Being possessed gives you a different outlook on these things.

Perry was getting angry. "You have the arrogance of the human race, Agent Katani. Which says any life form that is not convenient does not deserve to live."

Katani shrugged. "Your existential approach doesn't concern me. I track regenerates by the blood trails they leave."

"So there are other ones, like Erebus?" Lavee asked.

Katani looked over at her. "Yes, and when you work for the government, that kind of thing keeps the budget money flowing. It's better for the government to clock this and keep track. It keeps the funding flowing so that I can discreetly keep the body count down when they start going after their families."

"So you just slap a label on Erebus and write him off?"

"Any sympathy I had burned out a long time ago. So, no, ma'am, I'm not writing your husband off. I'm going to hunt him down and kill him. Now, have I got your permission to exhume the grave of your late husband, Erebus Lynch?"

"Evidently you don't need my permission."

"No, I don't need your permission. But I want it. And do I have your permission to track him down and remove this danger from your family? Or do you want him coming back again and again until he kills you and everyone else in your family with whom he has a strong connection? Your son. Your daughter-in-law. Whoever this Ray guy is?"

"He's my *husband*."

"I just want you informed on what is going to happen here."

She narrowed her eyes. "You going to do that by the dark of the moon?"

Katani gave her a steady look. "Daylight's better."

She closed her eyes and sighed. "You know, I really *don't* want to be here. Just give me a call and let me know what you find, Agent Katani. I think I've had enough."

I offered her my arm. "Let me walk you to your car, Mrs. Lynch."

She gave me a wary look. A look of dread. Waited to speak until we were out of earshot. "Katani is just as brutal and dangerous as I feared. Once he's murdered my husband, he's going to target my son."

"Jesse is safe. Katani won't hurt him; I'll make sure of it," I said, and hoped that I was telling the truth.

With Lavee Lynch gone, the tension eased. This was bad enough without her watching.

I spelled Katani with the digging, which went pretty fast—the ground was already churned up—then Perry took over, and I sat under the tree, pulled off my dirt-encrusted gloves that I normally used for gardening, not exhumation, and watched. Perry and Katani were digging now, all of us under the direction of Chloe who was taking samples as we went. She had the air of a researcher who has hit the jackpot.

It didn't take long. Erebus Lynch had done the heavy lifting when he'd clawed his way out. Something I wished I could stop thinking about. I looked up, saw something moving a ways away. A groundhog, up on its legs, watching us. The groundhog sign of alarm. We hadn't gone unnoticed.

A dirty, shredded shroud was balled up four feet down.

But that was all. None of us were surprised to find the remains of Erebus Lynch missing from his burial site.

"Confirmed," Katani said. "Ten forty-five a.m." He made a note of the date, time and location for his files.

I got up, took a shovel, and helped him put everything back. He was deft at smoothing the grave back down. Like a man who had done this kind of thing before.

And I wondered how many regenerates had woken up in a place where they couldn't get out of.

TWENTY-NINE

It was time to set up a master plan.

Perry and I had arranged to meet Jesse and Lola at the Grounded All Day Cafe—*A Gem in Historic Meadowthorpe.* The neighborhood brought back memories of my best friend from eighth grade who lived in Meadowthorpe, and the low-key trouble we used to get into back in the day. We could walk from his house to the Meadowthorpe Cafe, which was shut down years ago. We were always hungry back then.

The neighborhood has changed but it still feels the same. A little worn but sturdy. Antique stores, a billiards place. Apollo Pizza with its black and white mural covering an outside wall of singer-songwriter John Prine, much loved in Kentucky, and approved by his wife, Fiona Whelan Prine. A Marathon gas station that had stood for years on the very same spot. Stuttgart Auto Repair. New same-old, same-old grocery stores, restaurants, and houses going up just past the stoplight in front of the subdivision of old brick Cape Cods. The Meadowthorpe elementary school, everyone welcome. It's retro cool.

I took a moment to drive down the streets of the neighborhood, pass by in front of my friend's house, but that family was long gone. I wondered why we lost touch and where he was today, and I felt nostalgic for the life I had then, as much as I love the life I have now.

It made me late.

Inside there was a sign that said THIS IS THE PLACE. Perry was already there, and so were Jesse and Lola. They were eating bagels and the ambience of the cafe had done its magic. Jesse and Lola were smiling and they looked light and happy, not weighed down like I expected them to be.

Perry was smiling at them and listening. I waved, and got my favorite. An authentic, hand-rolled, shipped-in-from-NYC bagel—French onion cream cheese, shredded chicken, tomato vinaigrette, pickled jalapenos, crispy onions, and dressed greens. Toasted. A cortado—espresso and steamed milk made with Nate's Coffee—another local gem.

Perry was sipping his usual Cubano: espresso with sugar.

I stopped by the table and Lola looked up and smiled at me. "Look at this. I can eat. Their bagels actually settle my stomach. I've had two bagels and a hot chocolate."

"Want another one?"

She tilted her head to one side. "Actually, I do."

"Anyone else?"

Takers all around, so I added the hot chocolate, another Cubano for Perry, and a banana pancakes espresso for Jesse—banana, salted caramel, and maple.

I heard laughter when I was up at the counter, and when I sat down at the table, Jesse gave me a big grin.

"Have you heard the news?" he asked.

"Don't think so," I said.

Perry nudged me. "He doesn't get out much."

Jesse scrolled on his phone and brought up the *Louisville Courier Journal* with a screaming headline, literally, showing a headless ghost: "*Phantom of the Opera* gets real in Lexington for new musical *Bad Dad Tango*."

Ghost tourism was big in Kentucky, one of the most haunted places in the world.

Jesse leaned forward. "Word got out about what happened at the Manchester Music Hall rehearsal, the video of the attack is all over the place, and we've gone from a handful of tickets sold to completely sold out. You've still got the tickets I gave you, right? If not I'll be sure you get in."

Lola laughed. "We've got interviews set up on local news shows, our Instagram account got three thousand followers up from seventeen in *one day*."

They were both clearly ecstatic. I felt my stomach tighten and I looked at Perry who could read me like a book.

"Are you worried, Dr. Archer?" Lola asked kindly. Lola, of the recent close-call head injury, still looked thrilled. "Perry warned us you would . . . you would not be happy about this."

I would have to tread carefully. "I know how exciting this is, to have sold out the performances, and to see your play become a big success. But this is going to draw him in. It's going to bring him to the theater, and after what happened last time, you have to know how risky this is. Can you tell me your thinking on this? You already know mine."

Perry put his empty coffee cup down. "I think we can all agree, Noah, that this rock opera, *Bad Dad Tango*, is a form of very personal very private exorcism. It's therapeutic."

"Good theater always is," Lola said.

Perry nodded. "And the healing will come for Jesse and Lola, which is how this is meant to be. So that's not nothing. It does mean all hell is going to break loose. But Lynch is out there already, he shows up whenever he wants to, and if we draw him out on our terms, we can be ready. I think we go on the offense and don't wait to see one horror after the next. I think we take charge. This is war, Noah. It always is. So it's time for us to get proactive and end it if we can, as gently and kindly as possible—before Katani gets there first."

I had forgotten what a warrior he was. He liked having the upper hand.

Jesse leaned forward. "I'm not going to let my father take over my life again. And he's damn close to doing that now. But I'm not a kid, and I'm not under the thumb of my mother, and for better or worse, I don't see a choice.

"And the good news is my panic attacks have stopped. So far anyway. Not once since you told me what was really going on with my dad, and I thank you for that. I think it's because now Lola and I know what we're dealing with. And we'll do what we do, and it may be wrong, it may blow up on us, but let me tell you our plan before you make up your mind."

"Jesse, I can't tell you what to do."

"But you can advise us. And that's what we want. Because you're the one I really trust."

And I knew he meant it. So I listened. And he made a lot of sense.

"It helps that I'm not conflicted about my dad anymore," he said. "I used to lay awake at night feeling guilty when I was little, because I knew in my heart I didn't love him. I love Ray, no question, but not my dad. I think something inside me knew not to trust my dad, even back then. And I will always see this as a strength, an intuition I had even when I was a kid. He was mean to my mom, who protected me but always made excuses for him. He never wanted to come home to us, he didn't want a son. He didn't want kids. He always used to tell people, right out, that family was a weight that kept him from finishing school, taking that basketball scholarship, leading the life he was meant to have. And that he would be sure his son *did* have that life. But it was his life, not mine.

"And you know what? To me a family is everything. You don't always get to say how it will turn out, but ditching your family because you think they hold you back—that just proves what an entitled, narcissistic jerk my dad is. The older I get, the more I see him as a failed human being. I was relieved when he died. I'm not happy that somehow he's back. I get the biology you explained, and OK, if you say so. He's here so you must be right. It's hard to wrap your mind around. And so . . . I had a talk with Liam."

"Agent Katani?" I asked.

"He's a hard-ass," Lola said. "And he's ruthless. But it's empowering, because we know that Jesse's dad is going to show up at the Opera House on opening night, and so will Agent Katani. He's going to take him down—and we want to let him."

"You know what that involves?" I said.

Jesse nodded. "I do. Not as hard a decision as you might think. All I have to do is play that video of him picking Lola up and slamming her to the ground—"

Lola's smile faded.

"And when I see that, then I have zero doubt. If Agent Katani doesn't take my dad down, I will. No mercy."

I looked at Perry. "You're on board with this?"

"With the caveat that Jesse and Katani give you and me a chance to take Erebus to safety and help him."

"How so? The last exorcism didn't go so well."

"You know as well as I do it can take more than one. That it is like peeling away layers."

"Yeah, but with Erebus Lynch it makes him more and more dangerous and at some point we have to draw a line and say it isn't worth the risk. And I think we've more than reached that point."

"Exactly," Perry said. "But I want to try one more time. I'll do it safely, and then if it doesn't work, we turn it over to Katani. Because Katani is right—we can't let Erebus Lynch come after his family. We have to make that stop."

"And what if it works, Perry? What will we do with him? How will we keep working with him safely?"

"I—"

"You're thinking a mental health care facility?"

He nodded.

"So . . . incarceration?"

Perry sighed. "Not everybody sees these things the way you do, Noah."

"Because not everybody knows the reality of how this works. It would be a medical cruelty, Perry, because there are no good health care options for Erebus Lynch, and to store him in a mental health facility won't do him any good, even if it makes *you* feel better."

"Whose side are you on?" Lola said.

"*Yours*. With ethics."

"You don't think it's ethical to let Katani," she did finger quotes, "manage his death?"

"Absolutely not. And I don't think locking him down in a mental health care facility is either."

She stopped cold. Looked at Jesse. "OK, I'll say it. Honestly, I want to let Katani handle it. Better for him, better for us. The most important thing is to make sure he doesn't come back, and Katani said he knew how to take care of that. No offense, but I don't trust that either you or Perry do."

"I agree the cycle of resurrection needs ending. I just think we should do it with as much kindness and dignity as we can." I was thinking of the winch. Since they were saying 'managed death' I was pretty sure Katani hadn't explained that part.

Perry looked at me. "I still think we should offer him a chance first. See if he wants help."

I understood where he was coming from. As a medic, I wanted to be able to save Erebus, to try to heal him despite his crimes against his family. To make sure he faced justice in this world for what he'd done to Frankie. But the man in Erebus's skin was no longer him; there wasn't anyone left to save. And even if the tiniest part of Erebus remained inside him, what kind of a life could he live now?

"Sure, Perry," I said. "And are you going to agree to spend a couple of weeks in lockdown and restraints—chemical and physical—to get a feel for what life will be like for Erebus Lynch? It'll have to be Eastern State Hospital; that's the only facility that will admit a patient in restraints."

"I would if it would help, Noah."

"There is no way to make that work, Perry. And rainbow-and-unicorn thinking is dangerous. There is not much I can do to help him, and even if I could, you're all ignoring one thing. He cannot make a rational decision. Not possible. Your father is dying, Jesse. I don't think he has that long. His rate of deterioration is accelerated, and it's just a matter of time until he dies again. And we'll need to find him when he does. And if we *don't* manage his death, we risk him coming back and this starting all over again. Bad enough for you and Lola, Jesse, but believe me. *Hell for him.*"

Dead silence at the table.

"What do you advise then?" Jesse asked.

"Let's set it up. Perry is right: we can't just wait around and let him have the upper hand. So, let's be ready to have Katani capture your father at the Opera House. You and Lola will be onstage, it's opening night. You'll be nervous but that's normal anyway. I'll talk to Agent Katani, and I'll work with him on this.

"To be clear. I won't agree to go along with Katani's brutal methods, but the end game is the same: a managed, peaceful death for your father, and cremation so he does not come back again. And, Perry, if at some point we've got him cornered and rounded up, and you think we have a shot of helping him, then OK. If you can put his soul at peace before the death and the cremation and you think it's safe for you to try, then yes, do that. You'll have to decide if you're ready for the outcome to make things worse. So take some time to think it through, all of you, and let me know when you decide how to go."

"I've decided," Jesse said. "We'll do it your way. So long as Lola is OK with it."

She cocked her head to one side. "Just so long as the result is he *winds up dead*. And stays that way."

"Perry?"

"Just let me be there, Noah. This is not about brain damage. This is about spiritual turmoil."

"One other thing we need to cover," Lola said, and exchanged a glance with Jesse, who turned to frown at me.

"Where do you think he goes, my father? When he's not terrorizing my wife?"

It was a very good question.

THIRTY

FROM THE COURIER JOURNAL, LOUISVILLE, KENTUCKY

PHANTOM OF THE OPERA OR NIGHT OF THE LIVING DEAD?

Maybe both?

Has Erebus Lynch come back to life?

In Lexington, Kentucky, known for ghost tourism and one of the most haunted places in the world, with more ghosts than New Orleans, there have been sightings of a man who is officially dead. And in Lexington, the Opera House Theater has exceeded expectations. *Bad Dad Tango*, a rock opera about how fathers haunt their sons, has evidently called back the father of one of the writers of the play, penned by Jesse James Lynch, and his wife, internationally known saxophone player, Lola Strickler.

The opera deals with the existential issues of a man coming to terms with his own father, as he prepares to become a father himself. Jesse Lynch says he and his wife decided to write the opera to deal with the issues Lynch had dealing with the memories of his overbearing father, who often said that a wife and children inhibited him and weighed him down, and who died of lung cancer when Lynch was fourteen.

His goal? To be the kind of father he wants to be, not the kind he had.

"It's about how a father haunts a son," Jesse Lynch said. "I was thinking the haunting was more on an existential level—" Lynch smiles at me and laughs. "But then I started seeing my father. His ghost, his whatever. His presence, like he's come back to life." He shakes his head. 'Look, don't ask me to explain this. Somehow this rock opera has . . . called him back? I honestly don't know what's up with this. My wife and I are expecting twins, and I could not be happier. But I have this fear . . . this fear that instead of being the father I always wanted to be, I'll be more like him. It's not like I don't have a good role model. My stepfather, Ray, is exactly the kind of father I want to be. And it's also about understanding my father. Why he would say the things that he did. Why he even thought that was OK. What kind of man he was."

According to Lola Strickler, "Writing this play was a way for Jesse to work the issues through in a way that was fun, and creative, and we've had such a blast working together on this. Jesse is new to performing, but you'd think he'd been doing it all of his life. He has an ease and charisma onstage that is stunning. I have been performing since my teens, and I have been blown away by his presence onstage. Everything was going great, until his dead father actually showed up. I have never been so terrified in my life."

She nods her head, when I confirm that the ghost of Erebus Lynch attacked her during rehearsal at the Manchester Music Hall. "It's on video," she said. "Someone has set up an Erebus Lynch sightings YouTube channel. It's unreal. We've hired security for the shows, put a warning out to the audience, and we were afraid we'd get cancelled because of that, but it's just the opposite. People can't wait to see this and the Opera House isn't backing down. They have a history of supernatural events, and they are taking it in stride, but this may be one for the books." She smiles, showing a dimple. "That's how we roll in Kentucky. We're eccentric here. Everything is out there, our crazy families and our ghosts. It's not that we don't have anything to hide. It's just that we put it all out there."

The Opera House has put out a press release saying they will have increased security during the run of *Bad Dad Tango*.

Opening night is Friday, September 24th.

Tickets to all of the shows are sold out, but there is talk of extending the run.

Y'all come.

THIRTY-ONE

It didn't feel like work. It felt like the best night out ever. We went together, Moira and I, Perry and Chloe, and Liam Katani who was slicked up and handsome in freshly pressed jeans, loafers, a grey crew-neck sweater. He left us in the lobby.

"My guess is Erebus will come from backstage. Back of the theater. He'll be spooked by the crowds out front, and there's security everywhere. But he'll find a way in, I think. If not, he'll be around. I'll hunt him and find him, get a tracker on him, and then take him down."

"Won't security try to hand him over to the police?"

Katani patted the pocket where he kept his badge. "Department of Justice overrules. As soon as I see him, I'll text you. It would be great if you could come round back and be there."

"I could come with you now."

"No, we can't predict where he'll come in. Jesse and Lola will be onstage, I expect him there, just like the rehearsal at the Manchester. I'm well-armed, Noah. I've done this before. Don't worry."

I nodded. Made sense.

He left us once we were through the door.

Chloe had filled me in on Katani. She worried about him. He'd spent most of the years since getting his PhD on the road drifting with his job, and seemed lonely and untethered. Different from my initial take that he was a blowhard pain in the ass. But she'd known him since he was seventeen. And he did seem a little awkward and vulnerable with us, but he warmed up to Moira right away. Most people do.

The house lights dimmed, and Moira grabbed my hand and smiled. She was looking pretty in a tight black skirt and black sweater, hair piled on her head. She was always looking pretty.

"This is the perfect theater," she said, bending close.

She was right.

Built in 1887, with just under a thousand seats, it's one of the smallest theaters in the country hosting Broadway shows, but the nineteenth-century charm makes it a unique and popular venue. There are two balconies with boxes on either side of the stage. Seats upholstered with Turkish embroidery and Moroccan velvet.

Every seat was full, and the crowd was excited, whispering, looking over their shoulders. For a haunted theater, it had great, upbeat energy.

A spotlight hit the stage and the chatter stopped. Amps. A guitar propped against a wooden stool. A standing microphone.

Maybe three minutes, then I saw him.

Jesse James Lynch came in left of stage and settled on the stool, adjusting his microphone and guitar. He wore tight jeans, a black sweater, and a worn black leather bomber jacket. He shrugged the jacket off his shoulders and hung it over the back of the chair.

Jesse had an easy but mesmerizing presence. He turned and faced the audience. Looking at us as we looked at him. From my vantage in a front-row seat, his eyes looked electric and blue. His hair was parted to one side, thick, and he reminded me of the fifties rock and roll movies my mother used to love to watch late at night on old movie channels. She'd let me stay up and watch with her, and we'd cook a frozen pizza, and she'd have a glass of wine and I'd have a Coke. *Jailhouse Rock*. *Rebel Without a Cause*. *On Any Sunday* with Steve McQueen. My father had just died and this was our Friday and Saturday night escape.

Jesse strummed the guitar one or two times, and began to speak. His voice was solid. Steady. He had charisma onstage and I was impressed.

"Hey," he said. Primed and ready, the audience cheered, and he grinned. "Glad to see you too." He strummed a few chords, looking thoughtful, then leaned toward the microphone.

"I never got along with my father."

A whistle and some applause from the audience.

He smiled and looked out across the stage. "*Nooooo*. You too?"

Laughter.

"I grew up under the obsessive codependency of a flawed and dangerous man. Under the protection and judgment of a magical mother who looked out for me, made excuses for him, and never held him accountable for the things he said and did. He never wanted to be a father. He never wanted to be a husband. He spent his whole life trying to break free. Unhappy staying, afraid to go. I look to my parents and see them as the human beings they were, doing their best and doing their worst and my question is . . . will I do better? Because I'm going to be a girl dad soon. To twin daughters."

The applause was enthusiastic and he smiled and waited for it to die down.

"So I will take you with me on my journey of memory and understanding, not to vilify my parents but to understand them so that I can learn and do better. To understand what it is to be a good husband, a good father . . . a good man."

His voice was solid. Steady. I was so riveted, I almost forgot about Erebus Lynch.

Almost.

"Let's start with my mother and father. Their marriage was a mess, but there was no question that my father loved her more than anything on earth."

The spotlight moved behind him, and there they were. The actors who were playing Lavee and Erebus. Jesse began to play and they danced.

The song he played and sang was Johnny Cash's version of "One", the lyrics bitter, intimate, full of accusation and despair. Jesse's voice was golden, resonant. The dance was a push-pull of attraction and rejection. I looked at Moira, who was mesmerized.

The dancers froze. The spotlight moved to Jesse, who nodded at the applause and the actors disappeared behind him in the darkness of backstage. I could see the stagehands, all in black, moving across the stage.

No sign of Erebus.

Yet.

Then. Dark stage, spotlight on Jesse, sitting on a stool

sideways from a battered old recliner. Softer spotlight on his father, sitting in a chair in front of a silent television. The actor who plays Erebus looked like him, but he was younger, hair a blonde white. Still. They looked a lot alike.

I looked him up in the program. Arnie Young. No aspirations to Broadway or what was left of Hollywood. Some stints in European streaming horror movies. Happy with community theater right here in Kentucky. A breath of fresh air.

I shifted in my seat. When the real Erebus arrived, would Agent Katani be ready for him? Would he take the bait we'd laid?

I felt a stab of unease. So many people in the audience. Jesse and Lola onstage. The babies vulnerable in her belly. If this didn't go as planned . . .

And Jesse, onstage, revealing the intimacies of the kind of life so many of us had. Flawed parents, a father who made him practice basketball for two hours every day after school, a father who didn't want to come home at night, a mother who went from hurt to not *wanting* him home at night, both of them running in place in middle-class lock-step dysfunction.

In other words, Jesse said onstage to laughter, "A pretty typical life."

I got a text alert. It was Liam, letting me know that nothing was happening, all was well, he was watchful.

I didn't expect Erebus yet. Not until the key moment.

"Everything OK?" Moira whispered.

I nodded. Looked back up at the stage. Tried not to let my rising fear that I'd misjudged the situation overwhelm me.

Jesse strummed his guitar, leaned into the microphone as a picture was projected to a screen onstage.

"That's my mama, Lavee, barely twenty years old, at their simple wedding, a cake and punch reception in my mama's church. My dad wearing his Sunday suit, and my mom in a discount bridal gown. Both of them so young. They'll be parents of two sons in seven months, and mourn the loss of one of those sons only five months later. I wish sometimes I could go back in time and warn them. They were young then. Innocent. Until the life they had made them hard.

"My dad and my mom both had to drop out of college, and my dad worked long hours managing a grocery store chain, and he was good at work. He opened stores of his own and made a lot of money. He never came home for dinner, even after he got rich, and my mom would leave a plate of supper on the stove for him, with Reynolds Wrap over the top, to keep it warm. For my father, the hours between six and eight were mistress time. It took me years to figure that out but Mom knew. Mom knew everything.

"When we heard the garage door go up, we knew he was home, and my mom would retreat to the bedroom and shut the door. My father had a lot of bad moods and I could tell when he walked up the steps to the bedrooms what kind of mood he was in. Dragging his feet but walking hard, like a man who wanted to be anywhere else.

"I always wondered why he came home. Every night when I heard him dragging his feet I wished he'd never come home. To this day, when I hear a garage door go up, I feel sick to my stomach. I wasn't afraid of him. Ever. But I hated him. And every night I would stand in the hallway waiting for him. Hands in fists. Because sometimes a kid knows what he's not supposed to know.

"Then he would go to the bedroom, and I would hear the low tones of my parents talking long into the night. I would hear my mother cry. He liked telling her where he'd been and what he'd done. But one day I noticed that my mother stopped crying. She started buying him pack after pack of those little cigars with the white tips, he loved those—and yes, he inhaled, and he would smoke a pack and a half a day.

"I once heard her talking to a girlfriend, they were in the kitchen drinking Coke."

The lights dimmed, then focused on two women sitting at a small kitchen table.

I rely on the surgeon general, Jesse's mother said.

He says smoking is a death sentence. The girlfriend has big hair. Olive capri pants that reach a few inches below her knees.

I know.

Why not divorce him?

And let him have half custody? Time with my son with me not there?

Jesse signaled the band, which began to play while the two women danced. An Amy Winehouse song. "You Know I'm No Good".

The spotlight went back on Jesse.

"My father died of lung cancer when I was fourteen. I remember my mom and me side by side at his funeral visitation, people lining up for a quiet word, a lot of them women who knew my father a little too well.

"But there was one man there who stayed close, exchanging looks with my mom. He rode a motorcycle, and played electric guitar, and wore a black leather jacket. He had a lot of money from making small-batch bourbon that was all the rage in Kentucky. My mother decided at the last minute to skip the gathering of friends and family at the house after the funeral. Instead we went with the guy. Ray.

"He took us out for Mexican food and he and Mom had margaritas, and he talked my mom into letting me have one too. I was tipsy for the first time in my life.

"And Ray? He bought me my first electric guitar, could not get me to like bourbon no matter how hard he tried, but accepted my love for margaritas. *A tequila man*, he would say. We went to live in his apartment, which was over the warehouse where he made his bourbon. When I went to college, I could walk from there to campus at the University of Kentucky where I took every class I wanted. Guitar, Italian, ballroom dancing, playwriting, horseback riding, creative writing, painting, theater arts. I had a hell of a time and neither my mom nor Ray got upset when it didn't cobble together to make a degree. All that anxiety and dread I grew up with went away and was barely a memory. Ray taught me how to fix cars. Showed me how to love and cherish a woman.

"*He* taught me how to be a man.

"Some nights he and my mother would go outside on the rooftop deck—he had rigged up patio lights and had a firepit—and there is nothing more beautiful to me than a view of city lights in the darkness. One night, while they were drinking bourbon, she and Ray told me the rest of it. How Ray had gone to prison for killing his father after he found him beating his mother half to death. He was fifteen years old, tried as an adult. Gone for many years. Mama loved Ray, but she was young and she got lonely, met my dad, got pregnant with twins, and that's how I got made.

"My brother, Frankie, died at five months old. I've missed having a brother ever since." He looked up. "This is the song I always sing for Frankie. 'Summer's End' by the late, great John Prine."

The audience went quiet, mesmerized by the bittersweet lyrics.

Jesse let the guitar go quiet. "Twelve years ago, the most wonderful thing happened. I met Lola. My wife."

He moved right into "Wicked Game" by Chris Isaak.

The spotlight found her, beautiful Lola, wearing a black shimmery dress, hair shiny in the light, lips dark with red lipstick.

"I was a motorcycle riding bad boy, and she was a refined international musician. I didn't think she would have anything to do with me, and I had to chase her hard. But I got her to marry me, and she's pregnant now and as you know, we've got twins on the way."

Applause, cheers, and Lola crossed over to stand behind him, leaning close, smiling, arms around his neck.

"I want to be a good dad. The kind of father Ray is to me. I want to kill any part of me that is my dad. And with this play I challenged my father to get out of my life. I thought it was going to be existential. But you know, it didn't exactly work out like I planned. He's still haunting me and my mom. Every time we hear 'Moon River', his favorite song, it's like he's still here with us."

He grinned and the audience laughed and everyone felt nervous . . . including me. Erebus Lynch could show up any minute. And we all knew it.

The actors playing his mom and dad drifted in from stage right and began dancing in the spotlight as Lola picked up her saxophone and the haunting sound of "Moon River" rang out.

That's when I expected him. Erebus Lynch.

All the actors were onstage. Safe. Leaving the backstage area free for Erebus to arrive—and be intercepted safely and quietly by the lurking Agent Katani.

I texted Liam: Anything?

It took a few minutes to get the reply: I don't think so.

That worried me, but it was all I got.

By now the song was over, and I had missed some of the dialog.

"My father," Jesse was saying. "He still has a certain power over me I can't understand."

The band took up with a hard guitar beat, "Fast as You" by Dwight Yoakam, and Jesse and Lola danced the tango. The audience was clapping and whistling. Moira was holding my hand so tight it hurt. I was out of the moment, watching the audience, the aisles, the dark movements behind the actors onstage.

We were taking a hell of a risk. But every day with Erebus Lynch walking the streets was a hell of a risk. I just wanted it over with.

Jesse and Lola embraced after the dance. Jesse walked sideways holding her hand. Then he let her go, adjusted the microphone, and turned to the audience with a big smile.

"Ladies and gentlemen, I give you the amazing Lola Strickler, internationally renowned saxophone player, mother of my children, and my beloved wife."

His voice was solid. Steady. Despite the anxiety I knew he must be feeling about what might even now be happening backstage to his father. The two of them onstage together had a chemistry that was off the charts.

"They remind me of us, twenty years ago," Moira whispered, leaning close. Then she looked at me. "And you're going out of your mind with worry."

"I have to keep them safe."

But Erebus had not shown up as planned, and as he wasn't safely in Agent Katani's custody, I had no idea how I was going to do that.

THIRTY-TWO

Lola had picked up her saxophone again and I looked at the printed program to check the music she was playing. "Wiegala", a haunting lullaby written by Jewish poet and composer Ilse Weber. Bittersweet and beautiful, Weber composed the music and lyrics to sing to the children under her care when she was a nurse at Theresienstadt concentration camp. When they were sent to Auschwitz, she chose to accompany them and would not allow them to die alone. She sang this to them in the gas chamber, all of them holding hands in a circle, where they died together, the children not knowing what was coming.

Loving them through.

The works of Weber would have been lost to time, in the way the world refuses to embrace the creations of women. But her husband had gathered it all together, buried it in a box, and gone back years later to bring it home. His gift to the world. His gift to his much-beloved wife.

Love, no matter what. This was what Lola was telling Jesse.

I reached out and took Moira's hand, and finally the text I'd been waiting for came through from Katani.

Following blood trail. Get the actors offstage.

But Moira saw him before I did. Before I had time to react.

Erebus Lynch, coming down from the balcony, heading into the aisles between the seats, soaked in blood. Whose blood, I wondered.

Someone screamed, and Jesse jumped off the stage, running toward his father.

"*Jesse*," Lola screamed.

But there was no stopping him.

Katani was right behind him, blood smeared on his sweater, but he didn't seem hurt, and he was accurate and fast with the Taser.

Lynch staggered and roared and turned toward Katani, but Jesse tackled him and brought him down. Katani used the Taser again but it had the opposite effect. Lynch was up on his feet, confused and in a fury of fear and sensory overload. He swiveled, turning away from the stage and heading out of the theater, toward the lobby, Katani right behind him. People were scrambling out of their seats, holding up phones to record, and screaming. Security didn't try to stop people from leaving; they were smart enough to try and get them organized and orderly.

I saw Perry, heading in from the side of the theater. He looked pale and shaken. "Noah? You need to come."

I took Moira's hand. "Stay close. No daylight between us."

Jesse was coming toward me, and now he had Lola with him. "Somebody said something's happened to Arnie."

"He was the actor playing your father?" Perry asked.

Jesse nodded.

"I'm sorry," Perry said. "It's bad."

Security had blocked the hallway when I made it down to the dressing rooms. Perry had told them I was a doctor. They'd called paramedics and police, both on their way.

The uniformed woman who was in charge was shaken, as were all of them, milling in the hall. She shook her head. "OK, you're a doctor, you can go in, if you want. But he's already dead."

I went through the partially open door. The actor who played Erebus Lynch, much younger, but tall and slim, was hard to recognize. Most of him was still sitting in his chair. His head, however, was sideways against a wall.

Lola was crying softly when I went back out to the hallway.

"I'm sorry," I said. "No hope." I looked at Jesse. "Any texts from Liam?"

Jesse shook his head. Looked at Lola. "Want me to take you home?"

"No. You need to find Liam. You can't leave him alone with this."

I checked my phone. Nothing since the last text. I tried to call.

"Noah," Moira said. "Do you hear that?"

Liam Katani's phone. In a corner of the dressing room, smeared with blood.

I frowned. "We know he was alive earlier; we saw him chasing Lynch. Let's not underestimate him, but we do need to find him. Lola's right, we can't leave him alone with this." And something hit me. "Jesse. Where is your mother?"

"She and Ray were in the audience. They had tickets. She sent Lola a bouquet of flowers for opening night. She . . ." He trailed off. "I haven't seen her since . . . I mean, she was here earlier. You think she's OK?"

"Remember when you asked me where your father goes to ground?"

He looked stunned. "She'd know, wouldn't she? And Liam will be following him there."

THIRTY-THREE

I didn't want to separate from Moira, but she was adamant about heading home to the kids. My mother was there with them, but she didn't like the vulnerability. Instinct, she said. I knew she'd be getting her Glock out of the gun safe.

Lola went home with Perry and Chloe, who grabbed my arm. "Find Liam. He's on the hunt, and nothing will stop him from tracking down Erebus Lynch. It's not what he'll do to Erebus that worries me—it's what Erebus will do to him."

"I'll find him. His name means *Lucky* Hunter, remember? He'll be OK."

But she wasn't convinced and neither was I.

Lavee Lynch had not answered the phone, even when it was Jesse who called. After dozens of attempts, I knew my first instinct had been right. She was costing us time. She wanted Katani dead.

She did not answer the door when Jesse knocked, but we knew she was there.

"I have the key code," Jesse said. "Ray's car is gone. But she'll be up there. Probably up on the rooftop patio. I've been thinking about how my dad's clothes are laundered. He wears those worn but freshly ironed shirts, buttoned tight at the neck. You think she's still doing his fucking laundry?"

I didn't answer. I preferred the version of Lavee Lynch who had severed her husband's hand.

She was up on the roof, just as Jesse thought, curled up in a wicker rocking chair in front of the firepit, a tepee of logs enveloped in flame. Holding a glass of wine in one hand, and a half-full bottle in the other.

She glanced at us over her shoulder. Didn't seem surprised. "So good to see you, Jesse. Go get a couple more wine glasses from the kitchen, and you two sit down. It's chilly—a good night for a fire."

She was playing for time.

"Where's Dad? Agent Katani is following him, so where does he go to ground? We've got Katani's phone. He managed to get a tracker on Dad, but the signal went out. On both ends—Katani and Dad."

"Please know that I didn't leave the theater until I knew you and Lola were safe. It was a wonderful show, Jesse. You are such a talent. But once I saw your dad, I asked Ray to take me home. It was just . . . my nightmares coming true. I have compassion for Erebus, and now the whole world has seen who he is. He was such a fucked-up mess of a man, even back then, in his prime, buying into the idea that he was entitled to fuck any woman who looked his way, to devote himself to his job, and to look at us like we were a weight around his neck. It didn't make him happy. He never found his way. And I would write him off if I could, but . . . do you see him now? How vulnerable he is? A monster . . . or a man?"

"Why do you do it? Iron his shirts and give him a place?"

"So he'll be dependent on me, Jesse. So that when things go wrong and he's in a fury, he'll come after me rather than you. And it means I can keep an eye on him. Find him if I need to. Agent Katani says your father is a monster. He is not factoring in that he was *always* a monster. A monster you loved—whether you still do, I don't know, and maybe you don't know either, you don't have to think about that."

"Oh, I think about it."

"So this is business as usual for me. I have always had to deal with Erebus. If I could kill him forever, I would, but I tried, and I failed. This is strategy, Jesse. I've always dealt with your father this way. You wouldn't be so shocked if you were thinking this through."

But I was. "Keep your enemies close?"

She nodded, looking at her son. "Once he died and came back, I knew I'd never be free. But he'll have to go through me before he gets to you and Lola. And I am formidable."

"Where is he, Mom? Where's Ray?"

She stared into the fire as if Jesse wasn't there. "Ray knows what to do. Better you're not involved."

Jesse picked up his phone, called Ray. Had a short conversation, and I saw it in his face. Shock and determination.

"We need to go. Ray already found them. He says Agent Katani is hurt, he's bleeding out. He called an ambulance, but it may already be too late. He's doing what he can."

"Katani is a danger to you, Jesse," Lavee cried. "Tell Ray to just let him die. Dr. Archer—"

I didn't hear the rest. I was already in a sprint for the car, heading down the stairs of the condo, moving fast, Jesse right behind me.

"Where are they?"

"They're in a storage unit down the road from your office, just past the distillery warehouse. Two miles tops. I have no idea what the fuck they're doing there, but we have to move."

"Give me the phone."

Ray was on the line immediately. "Dr. Archer? I've called 911."

I heard moans of pain. Bad pain. Katani.

"Jesse said you told him that Katani is bleeding out. Put pressure on the wound, anything, rags, your shirt, your jacket, and just keep adding layers and pressure—and I mean press down hard and don't let up. Where is the wound?"

"Thigh."

Femoral artery. "Is the blood spurting?"

"It was, but not now. I've been trying to get it to stop," he said, sounding strained.

"That's something. Sounds like you're doing great. Just keep the pressure on, hard pressure, don't let up, I'm on the way. With any luck the ambulance will get there first. But I'm only three minutes away."

"I'm not sure he has that long."

Neither was I. Katani would have a total of five minutes till bleed out. Odds were he'd be dead by the time we got there.

"I need to know what we're walking into," I said as we dashed down the stairs toward my car. "Erebus?"

"Gone. For now." Ray gave me directions so we could find the unit. It would be lit up, door open, easy to find.

More time slipping by.

I drove. Jesse's hands were shaking, hard. It was dark out, a rundown place, no codes to get in. We saw the stream of black-red blood seeping out of the open storage unit, lights bright in the darkness. Nobody else was around.

The units were metal, the doors a cheerful if fading candy-apple red, and this unit was one hard left turn from the entrance, the door wide open. Ten by thirty. Most of the space was taken up by the gold Cadillac that was haunting my dreams. Rented to Ducati Distillery, as I would later find out. We scrambled out of the car, then Jesse came to a halt just in front of me.

"Jesus," he said. "Liam."

The blood was everywhere. Ray's olive-green sweater looked black with it, and he was crouched down, pressing old towels and cleaning rags over Katani's left thigh, using his full weight to press them down hard over the wound.

Katani would have about twelve pints total, and from the looks of things he'd lost at least half, but the blood was just seeping now, slow and sluggish, as Ray had said. Progress.

Ray was focused and calm. "Should I step away to give you space?"

"No. Keep that pressure on the wound." I moved over to Katani. "Liam," I said, crouching close to him.

He moaned, head twisting from side to side.

I knelt down beside him. He was still breathing, eyes glazed but open.

"Can't feel my leg," he whispered.

"Hold on, OK? This is going to hurt, I'm sorry, but if you feel the pain, consider that good news." I looked up at Ray and Jesse. "Hold him. I need that leg in place; don't let it slide out from under me."

I crouched down beside him, positioning my right knee over the wound on his left thigh. Pressing harder and harder, Katani screamed—*good news*—and twisted sideways. He didn't have a lot of fight left. Jesse had his shoulders. Ray kept the leg in place. I kept pressing, I'd need a hundred and twenty pounds of pressure to stop the spurt of blood. Easy enough for a man my size.

"Nobody move until the emergency crew gets here."

Soon we could hear the truck pulling in, voices.

I slid my hand inside the wet flap of Katani's shirt, looking to check his heartbeat.

Nothing.

His eyes flickered. He was staring at me. And then I knew.

"Other side," he whispered.

I slid my hand to the right side of his chest. Got the sluggish beat of his heart.

"It's OK," I told him. "I'm not letting you die."

"If . . . I don't want . . ."

"Understood."

Agent Liam Katani was a situs inversus mirror twin just like Jesse, just like Erebus, just like the monsters he tracked. No wonder hunting them was his life's work. Now I understood why he was there to manage their deaths, and be sure they stayed dead, no matter what.

If he died, which was very possible, I would do the same for him.

And then I realized that Erebus Lynch's bolthole hadn't just been close. He'd been two miles from my office, breathing right down my neck.

THIRTY-FOUR

Ray had taken charge after Katani was packed into the ambulance, setting out three lawn chairs, giving me a wet towel for basic clean up, then opening a bottle of Ducati Heat single-barrel bourbon and pouring everyone a generous pull.

The storage unit had a water hookup, and he hosed the blood away, then peeled off his sweater, shoving it into an open trash barrel, revealing a blood-stained white Hanes tee shirt underneath, like the kind my dad used to wear. He settled down beside us and picked up his drink, studying the amber bourbon and swirling it slowly in the glass.

"Katani is in surgery," I told them, putting my phone back in my pocket. They would repair the artery and hopefully save his leg, give him copious blood transfusions. "Chances are excellent that he will keep his leg," I told them cheerfully. "He has a good surgeon. That makes all the difference."

I picked up my glass and took a slow sip, sighing with pleasure.

Ray was watching me with the hint of a smile. There is nothing on earth like small-batch single-barrel bourbon, which means no blending with other barrels. So it's going to be great or it's going to be bad, nothing to hide behind. Ducati Heat was one of the great ones—known for its high proof and intense flavor. A complex medley of warm vanilla, toasted walnut and hazelnut, a hint of butterscotch and maple.

I sipped it slowly, wondering if I'd ever have the energy to get out of this chair. I put the glass down before it was finished, because it was going straight to my head.

Ray sighed too. "Well, Jesse, I suppose you want to know what the hell is going on here."

"That I do." Jesse stared straight ahead. He wouldn't look at Ray.

"I know you're furious with me, son. All I ask is that you hear me out. Your mother and I rented this storage unit when it was new, about twenty years ago give or take. Your father had just died, you were fourteen, and she was in a panic about what to do about the car."

"The *car*?" Jesse said incredulously, giving Ray a look.

"Your father's Caddy."

"*That* was her problem? What to do with his car?"

"Don't apply logic, Jesse. Your mother was a mess when your father died. She was relieved that he was dead, had been trying for years to kill him off with those cheap cigars, and when she finally did, only then did she start to worry how you'd handle it. First she was thinking she should keep the car for you, for when you were old enough to drive. Then she decided it would be terrible for you to have it—anything to do with Erebus she thought was bad. I told her you were a motorcycle guy, you were already learning to ride on my old Ducati, and I was going to get you your own when you turned sixteen. Which I did."

Jesse nodded. "Then why keep that goddamn car?"

"Let me finish. I wasn't just looking out for you, Jesse, I was looking out for your mom. It was easier for your mother to just put everything she felt she should keep in this storage unit. Which came down to the Caddy and a stack of worn but laundered dress shirts. All of them white."

"That makes no sense," Jesse said.

I put a hand on his arm. "Grief and trauma never make sense until it happens to you. But if it made her feel better . . . if it got her through . . ."

Ray nodded. "Exactly right. She almost never came here, but I did, to start up the car regularly, take it out for drives, and keep it in shape. It was always a sweet ride. I had stuff here too. Some old tools—"

"A chainsaw?" I asked.

He nodded. "I know Lavee told you she killed Erebus when he came after her in our garage, but it was this place, not the condo, where he cornered her that first time. She'd been uneasy, because she thought she had seen him around the house, smelling the cigar smoke, seeing the car. She thought it was just a nightmare, a vision. Her fears getting hold of her."

Jesse let out a slow sigh. "Just like what's been happening to me and Lola."

Ray nodded. "Exactly like that. She went to the storage unit to get rid of his stuff, to finally let it all go. The car wasn't there and she figured I'd gone and gotten rid of it, we'd been discussing doing just that, and for a moment she felt happy, she felt free. I'd say she had a good three minutes with the weight of Erebus Lynch off her shoulders.

"She was rounding up the shirts and putting them into a trash bag when she heard something behind her. And then he was there. She turned around, and she said she knew he was going to kill her. She just knew. You know what happened. She was terrified; she grabbed the chainsaw off the wall. She cut off his hand—"

"And you put him back in his grave." Jesse frowned. "But why did she change her mind and keep his stuff, the shirts, the car? You could have gotten rid of everything after you . . . got rid of him."

"Because we didn't understand what had happened. How he came back. Still don't." He held up a hand. "Yeah, I've heard the explanations and I'd rather not think about it. But Lavee was terrified he'd come back again, and she figured he'd always come here first, a sort of touchstone for the familiar, and God knows he loved the car. So we kept it as a kind of early-warning system. We'd know if he was around. We'd know to look out for you. And besides, your mother *killed* a man here, there was blood all over the floor, the walls. We did our best to clean up, but it seemed too risky to hand the unit back. What would we tell the police if they came by—that yes, your mom had killed a man in that unit, but they weren't to worry because he was already dead?"

"It never occurred to you to tell me?"

"*Every day*. But Lavee is your mother and I could see her point. Would you have believed her? Would you have spent your life looking over your shoulder, waiting for your dead father to show up?"

"If you think you spared me, you didn't. You made it worse."

Ray nodded. "I agree. And when he went after Lola—that was the end of the line for me. I told Lavee that you and Lola and I were going to have a talk, but then it wasn't necessary. Dr. Archer here took care of it."

"You should have told me all of it. And now he's back yet again and we need to deal with it—end it—once and for all." Jesse put his glass down. "Katani better live. He has some interesting insights. Because he hunts down people like my dad and he kills them. He admits that right out. And I see his point.

"He says Dad is alive and not alive. He doesn't eat, and eventually he'll starve to death. And maybe come back yet again, if conditions are right. And that thing he does . . . one minute he is six feet away, the next right in your face. Liam's seen it before. He said you think my dad might be the next step in human evolution, Dr. Archer. Me and Dad—"

"And Liam."

Jesse nodded. "He told me, before I went onstage. I think he felt he owed it to me, given he was about to kill my dad. He also thinks you might be able to help him. Help me. People like us. *Others*."

"Listen, Jesse. You are not other, unless all of us are. We all have our stuff. I can't save your dad. Katani was on the right track there. We need to find Erebus. Help him die with dignity. *I* was on the right track there. We need to make sure it doesn't happen again. That's all we've got. But you and Katani? Things will be different. I have hope."

"You have some magic cure for us up your sleeve?"

"If there was a magic cure, none of us could afford it, that's the way our health care system is, your money or your life. But cognitive decline comes to a lot of us. There are meds to mitigate it, ways to manage it. I have patients who deal with this every single day and still love their life. I do what I can medically and they take it from there. Some are miserable, some are OK, some are quite happy. It's just like everything else in the world. There are variables. Sometimes you can find a good way. Sometimes you can't, no matter how hard you try, and then you give up."

"Yeah. When I first found out, I felt like I didn't have a future. But there was Lola, and our babies are coming—"

"Of course you have a future," Ray said.

"And you'll keep an eye on me and if I ever become a danger to my family—I'll end it. And set it up so I don't come back."

"It's a good plan," I said. "You won't need it—but it's a good plan."

"So. My dad. We need to kill him before he kills us."

The decision we always came to. There was no other way.

"What does my father want with me, anyway?"

"To keep you for his own," Ray said.

Jesse shook his head. "Some things never change."

I stood up, gave them both a nod. "OK, guys. I'm exhausted and I'm going home after I stop by the hospital to check in on Liam. To be honest, from the way your father looked tonight, I think the next thing that will happen is his body will turn up. And then we'll have to move fast so he doesn't come back again. Don't let your guard down. He doesn't have long."

THIRTY-FIVE

Liam Katani was in obvious pain. His eyes fluttered when he saw me.

"Good news, Liam. You didn't need a graft. This will take some healing time, and some rehab, but you're going to be good as new."

He shut his eyes. Turned his head away. "No thanks."

"No thanks for what?" I pulled a chair up by his bed. "I got your test results, Liam. Lots of information in those fragments of bone they had to remove. From an old injury. You've been around . . . quite some time."

"I know you want to ask."

"If you want to tell me."

"It was the Santa Clarita woman. She broke my leg and she broke me. *I felt so bad for her*. She was so talented. She'd been a great mom, and she killed her own daughter. At the school. And she didn't even clock it, man, she was that far gone. I wanted to help her. I always wanted to help them. It's a nightmare, what we go through. I've always thought of myself as the mercy police. And . . . I let my guard down with her."

"That picture you showed me. The scars on your back."

"Yeah. The rest of the pictures were too gruesome to keep. I don't like looking at them, but I kept one to remind me to stay sharp. All of them taken while I was still alive, and in the hospital. I got myself out early in the morning. I got myself home. Locked up the house, left a note on how to dispose of my body. Laid down on the bed, took some pain pills, and went to sleep. I figured I wouldn't wake up.

"I lived alone, nobody checked on me. Somebody like me can't have a wife, a child. I don't even have a dog, even though I've always wanted one. My leg was broken; I had open wounds. I went into sepsis, my organs started shutting down. It happened surprisingly fast."

I nodded. Sepsis is a major cause of death with traumatic injuries.

"And then . . . I woke back up. My body turned back on, did its regeneration thing. Before anyone found me. To tell the truth, it pissed me off. I have never felt so alone in my life."

He opened his eyes, gave me a steady look. "We turn, you know. Like that Santa Clarita woman. I feel the darkness surrounding me, trying to get in my head. So far I've held it off. It's been a struggle. There are dark things out there. Opportunistic. Waiting to take us the Witchery Way."

"That why you take the antipsychotics? I clocked traces of them in your blood."

"Yeah man, they're a lifesaver."

"Your MRI doesn't look too bad. I'm not seeing a lot of cognitive impairment."

"Good to know. But I'm done, Dr. Archer. And since I'm going to die again," he said, "for once I'd like to make arrangements."

"You're not dying."

He sighed. "I'm actually in charge of that. I manage death for a living. I want to die fast, and I want to die now. I've already done the end-of-life paperwork, with instructions for a fast cremation. I'd have put everything I own in a trust for my sister, but I don't own anything. What I need you to do, Noah, is oversee that cremation and get it going within the next twenty-four hours."

"It happens that fast?"

"It starts that fast—and listen, it might not take; the auto-immune response goes more haywire every time. You're not going to like what comes back. I'm getting less and less human. Next time I won't be able to keep the darkness out, no matter how many drugs I take."

"You tell yourself that, Liam, but I like you just fine. You're not a monster, you're a man, and a good one. Don't talk yourself into a corner on this."

He ignored me. "It's all in the paperwork, in that cardboard box in my Tahoe. My personal stuff is at the bottom of the pile. I want you to make sure I am cremated and rush it, man, don't mess around. Please. I don't want to come back. I'm tired. I'm tired in my soul."

"Yeah. I'll do it. If needed. But, look, Liam, I cure autoimmune disease all the time. It can take a while; there's some trial and error, but—"

"You're not hearing me. I'm tired of hunting. I'm tired of being alone. I'm tired of being the grim reaper of mirror twins."

"You think Jesse needs to be hunted down?"

"Jesse? Hell no. He's got a wife; he's got kids on the way. He has a life."

"You could still have all of that. You could have a life that you love. Stay here in Lexington, make it your home base. Go to work for Chloe, write up your observations, keep monitoring. Keep taking the drugs. Father Cavanaugh and I will help you fight off the demons. You don't have to ride off into the sunset all alone and you don't have to die."

"*Tired*," he said softly.

"C'mon, man. You have this amazing ability to regenerate, and I can stimulate that and keep the autoimmune reaction under control."

He looked at me. Thinking.

"Why should you die? Because you're different? All of us are different. Should my patients with muscular dystrophy die? Should they have children? If their lives are shorter, does that mean their lives don't count? Because they *do* count. You act like dying is going to do the world a favor. As if you don't belong. As if—"

"*As if I'm trouble.*"

"We're all trouble, Liam. That's called being a human being. You could easily argue that you're the future. That you're the way humans are evolving—not devolving. Able to regenerate diseased or dead tissue—how can that be bad? Yes, right now it comes with complications. Vulnerability to cancer. Vulnerability to possession by dark spirits. Going into a cognitive decline that makes you violent."

"That's not just complications, that's—"

"But, Liam, life is a miracle and life is a mess. So if you are truly tired in your soul, and you don't want, say, another ten years, if there is nothing you want to do for another act in your life, then yeah. I'll take care of things. I will treat your remains with respect and make sure they stay dead. But why not give it a shot?"

"The hunt is all I know and I can't sleep knowing they are out there."

"Then find them. Help them. Help their families. But this time, do it before they die. Let them know what they're facing. Help them keep out the darkness. Find another way. Send them to my clinic; the Enlightenment Project is waiting for them."

"And then what?"

"And then *nothing*, your job is done. You don't make their decisions. I don't make the decisions for my patients. I tell them what they are up against, and with *my* patients? It's always formidable. I give them the options—they choose the path. That's why Jesse and Lola won't forgive Lavee. Because she took that away from them. Nothing less than the ability to decide the course of their lives."

"It just sounds so hard. Doing all of that."

He shut his eyes tight. I knew that he was hearing me, but not quite having it. It could go either way, and there was nothing else I could say. Except. I had something to show him and now was the time. His great-grandmother was right. I'd know when.

I was flooded with relief and a kind of peace. This was not up to me. This was over my pay grade, and so I'd give Liam Katani the message I'd almost forgotten I'd received, and leave the rest to the woman who still loved him and watched out for him.

"I have a message for you, Liam, from your great-grandmother."

He went very still. "What the hell are you talking about? My great-grandmother died a long time ago. You must be mistaken."

So I told him about the woman who'd mysteriously shown up on my porch, claiming to have a message for someone called Liam, and told me that I should take a photo of the two of us. Liam's eyes were open like slits of pain, but I had his interest. I pulled the picture up on the phone.

He took it out of my hand and studied it for a long time, whispering something I could not catch.

"Whose dog is that in the photo?" he asked finally. "Yours or hers?"

"Mine, but I have to say I think Tash would have followed her anywhere."

He smiled. "Yeah. Maudie—that's my great-grandmother—always had a dog at her feet, a cat in her lap, a horse on a lead rope. Possums in the yard, and groundhogs stopping by to dig holes in the yard until the dogs ran them off. One time, we were all out canoeing on the Tennessee River, me and Maudie and my sister and my mom, and damn if some dog didn't see her from the shore, jump in the lake and climb into the canoe. We took that dog home, an Aussie Shepherd that Maudie said called herself Roo. She always asked her animals what their name was. Even me. My mother had three baby names lined up, and she was going crazy trying to decide, and then Maudie held me and said, 'Oh, honey, this one is Liam.' My mom said, 'You don't get to name my child,' and Maudie said, 'This is the name he came with.'"

"Well, she gave me a message for you."

"Just the kind of thing Maudie would do. I was her favorite. I was always everyone's favorite." And there it was. That damn smirk.

"I wish you could have seen her back in the day. In fact . . . I think they put my wallet with my stuff somewhere."

I picked up the plastic bag on the chair. His wallet was black leather, slim and worn. Stained dark with his blood.

"Hand it here," he said.

He unfolded the wallet, flipped to the slot for credit cards and driver's license and his ID, and tugged a worn and creased picture out of a bottom slot.

"An actual picture," I said, as he handed it to me.

"Yeah, no cell phones then, this was back in the day when I was little. I want you to see the woman she was."

I studied the picture and smiled. Thick dark hair, piled on her head, loose, wavy, and spilling down her back, lush, rounded and her eyes so very blue. She held the bridle of a black draft horse, huge, and a little Liam was perched on the horse's back, so small his legs stuck sideways out over the sides of the horse.

"Me, Mamaw, and Wanda, the draft horse my grandfather had. She was huge and gentle and she would let me sit on her back and Maudie would lead us in a circle around the barn. I was forbidden to be up on that horse—my mother would have been furious—but Maudie and I had secrets. You can see the kind of woman she was. Not one to follow the rules. She had the courage of her convictions and she loved me like nobody's business."

"You look happy."

"I was always happy when I was with Maudie Belle. She and my mom squabbled off and on their whole lives, but when Maudie died, my mother grieved hard. So did I. I was lucky to have her."

"You still do."

He thought about that. "Text me the picture, OK."

I pulled out my phone. "Done. And she had a message for you."

He looked up at me steadily. "Tell me everything she said. Every word."

I shut my eyes, thinking. "She said I was supposed to meet you because like you I had walked the dark path."

"Have you?"

"I'm sure Chloe told you. I was possessed as a child, and it was only thanks to Perry that I survived it."

"Yeah. She told me that. Perry wouldn't talk about it, but Chloe and I are close."

"Yes, I know."

The smirk was back and for once I was glad to see it.

"Maudie talked about synchronicity and spiritual warfare. She asked you to remember the hero you were when you wouldn't let your mother cut her hair when she was ill."

He flinched. "She was so sick. Just wasting away. So thin and so fragile. Like you could break her if you didn't touch her soft. My mom was taking care of her at home, she didn't shut her away in some nursing home, but . . . I mean, it was hard for both of them. Washing Maudie's waist-length hair, it was a lot of work and bother on top of everything else my mom was doing. But I knew it would break Maudie if my mom cut it, like she was losing herself, that she would give up, and I didn't want her to give up, I wanted her to live. And my mom, I mean she got it finally. She cried and said OK, and that I was a hero."

"That's what Maudie said."

"Anything else?"

"She also said that I could raise the dead."

He glared at me. "Can you, then? OK. Do the treatments. Bring me back. If I come back dark and dangerous, we're both going to have a problem on our hands—but you more so than me."

I nodded. "If that happens, I'll take it up with Maudie myself."

"Dude. I will tell you as a kindness not to mess with my great-grandmother, dead or alive."

"Then do just one thing instead when you . . . wake up. Get a dog. You're the one that brought it up. It must be something you've thought about."

That stopped him. "Yes. I've always wanted a dog."

"There are plenty of them out there."

"A dog wouldn't be hard."

"Depends on the dog," I smiled. "But no, Liam, you're right. A dog is a great step."

"A dog is not a step. *You* have a dog."

"Of course I have a dog."

He grimaced, looked away. "I don't know. I just—"

"Find a life you love, Liam," I said gently.

He didn't speak for a moment. "Yeah. You're right. I'll give it a shot. I've always wanted my own dog and I'm going to get one. A puppy. Don't know where, don't know when, but I do know I'm going to name him Shrimp."

People who knew what they were going to name a dog when they got one had been wanting one for a long time.

"It'll work until he grows up—and then it'll work even better."

It was clear to me that Liam's pain was getting worse. He grimaced again. "Then it will just be funny. I think when we're not camping in the Smokies, he's going to be a very urban dog, and I might follow that hard trail I've never been on. See how far we get. It feels like something I need to do. Let go of the regret and go forward, no matter how it works out."

"What kind of dog are you going to get?" Because it was all about the plan. Getting a plan means getting a life. I didn't want him to give up.

"I think . . . let's just go with a dog. Don't box me in on this."

"He's going to be big. You need a big guy."

"In my line of work that's a good thing. I'm going to teach him to hunt."

I did not ask him what they'd hunt; I was afraid I already knew. "I had a great-uncle who had hunting dogs. They were the love of his life. He built them a two-story doghouse, heated and cooled. When they got old, he brought them into the big house."

"You are making that up. Nobody air conditions a doghouse."

"I am not making that up. My great-uncle just loved his dogs."

He took an uneven breath, his color growing even paler. "I'm not putting Shrimp in a doghouse. He's going to stay with me."

"No need to decide right now. Either way. You're in pain. Let me take care of that."

I administered the meds myself, sat beside him while they took effect. Saw the lines in his face ease, too young for lines like that. And too old. His breathing went from short, staccato beats of agony to slow peace. I sat until he was deeply asleep. Made sure he would have all the pain meds he needed. Wondered how old he really was. How many lives he'd really had.

THIRTY-SIX

But the night wasn't over yet.

Five minutes before I pulled into my driveway, my cell phone rang. I put it on speaker and heard Tash barking hysterically.

"*Noah*." Moira sounded shaky. "Erebus Lynch is on the sidewalk in front of our house."

I felt an electric jolt of energy and fear.

"The kids are in our bedroom, locked in with the cat and Tash. I'm downstairs in your office, watching out the window, and I've got my Glock."

"Call the police. I'll be there in three or four minutes. If he comes within ten feet of the house, be ready. And if you shoot, shoot to kill."

She took a breath. "Is this really happening?"

"Remember that thing I told you about? How he can be outside the window and then suddenly in the house, suddenly in your face? He did that at Lola's apartment. She had the balcony door shut and locked."

She caught her breath. "If he can do that, what's stopping him from going upstairs to the boys?"

"You, Moira. You'll stop him. But stay in the house. If he gets inside? Gets too close? No mercy."

"Define too close."

"If you can see him, take him out."

"I'll wind up in jail for murder, but that might be my only choice."

"No, we have a better option. We'll call Ray."

"And Ray is?"

"Jesse's stepfather. He's dealt with getting rid of Erebus more than once."

"What does he do?"

"He just rolls him up in a blanket and puts him back in his grave."

Moira laughed. "Brilliant."

"I'm on my way, sweetheart. Make sure you don't shoot me by mistake when I get home."

He was singing when I got there. "Moon River", the Erebus Lynch classic, something I was beginning to think of as his kill song. And I hated him for it. Hated seeing him with a cigar in his mouth, dancing down my sidewalk and close to my driveway, all the porch and security lights blazing. He had changed his shirt, but there were bloodstains on his trousers. I could not get the image out of my mind—Liam Katani bleeding out on the storage room concrete floor. My wife and two little boys in the house. I wondered if I should let the cat out. Cats did not like Erebus Lynch.

In the three minutes it had taken me to get home, I had made a decision to ignore my savior syndrome, which comes with surgeon territory. I would not give him one chance. I would not offer him help.

People in cognitive decline can seem terrifying when they are confused, and angry, and trying to make sense of a reality that does not match ours. But Erebus Lynch had somehow gone feral. His soul mingled with something dark, his body beyond repair. Not even Perry's exorcisms could save him. And it would be foolish and dangerous to try.

Mirror twin regenerates were a new human direction, Chloe had said. Which didn't make it good. Trying to reason with him, to help him, made as much sense as trying to talk down a grizzly bear. Lynch had an agenda that didn't make sense to me; he lived a life I could not figure out, and he seemed to exist both in my world and a shadow world where he could wander in and out.

And I was on his radar. He was in front of my house.

The scientist in me was fascinated. The doctor wanted to help. The husband and the father wanted to end him. Which is exactly what I'd do. If my wife didn't beat me to it. She was the one with the Glock.

* * *

The phone rang as soon as I turned my car engine off. Moira.

"I see you, Noah. Just stay in your car until the police get here; they're always fast. If he comes near you, I'll shoot his fucking head off. If nothing else it will shut him up and we won't have to hear him sing anymore."

"What I love about you, Moria, is knowing that you can."

"What are you going to do?"

"I'm going to come into the house with you."

"Too dangerous, my husband."

"I'm not sitting out here in the car. I've been stuck in a car with him once already and it's not something I intend to repeat."

"You never told me that."

"Forgot. See you in three minutes, baby doll."

I got out of the car slowly, leaving the door not quite shut—no loud and sudden noises. He was watching me. Still singing. He seemed calm. Pleased with himself, which pissed me off. I walked to the back of my car, a little closer to the house. Then stepped to the edge of the sidewalk, about twenty-five feet away, and waited while he watched.

He came closer, humming now. Shoulders loose, like a curious dog, face slack in a way that looked like dystonia. The muscles would not work anymore. He could not smile. Even if he wanted to.

I was not sure that he did.

It can't be an easy thing, coming back from the dead, and he'd done it twice—with no medication to halt his mental deterioration, his soul mingling with the dark. Who knew what exactly was inside his head. Whatever it was, it wasn't good.

He came to a hard stop, glared at me.

"Dude, don't come any closer. I'm going into my house to see my family and you're going to stay outside. I'll ask you nicely once to go sing and dance somewhere else. You're not welcome here."

And there it was. *The rage.*

Most patients in cognitive decline either can't control it or don't recognize it, or both, and I didn't want to push my luck. He was getting too damn close. If I ran, that would trigger his prey drive—or the prey drive of the dark force inside him. Either way, I had a feeling that it was strong.

"I understand the way it feels when people don't understand. When they look at you like you're a monster. When *your own son* calls you a monster. The son you love more than anything in the world."

He began to sway, stumbled sideways, splayed his feet in a stance I had seen before. Feet turned out in the way of someone who thinks they are going to fall, who knows their muscles cannot be relied on, and their legs can go right out from under them with no warning. Knowing it can happen anytime and anywhere, which turns walking into an act of courage. When they fall, they go down hard. Have trouble getting back up. Endure the exasperation of impatient, healthy people who would prefer to tie them down or drug them for what is determined to be their own good.

And it made me wonder if that ability to move as if by magic was a skillset developed in reaction to the ongoing danger of imminent falls, combined with the unknowable powers of the dark, unwelcome spirit that squatted inside his rotting body. Erebus Lynch, the next step in human evolution. Regenerating tissue, reinventing locomotion, consumed by rage, held together by something magically evil.

Sounded intriguing.

"Lynch. You keep getting closer and my wife is going to shoot you and I'm going to remove your brain and study it in my lab."

He hesitated. Took a step back. And I wondered if he was in pain—the remnants of the original man that had been Erebus, deep inside his core. So many of my cognitive patients were. It was almost impossible for them to say what or where the problem was when so many of their neural connections were shorted out. If he were my patient, I'd give him one of the newer antipsychotics, some gabapentin and a low dose of Ativan and morphine. If nothing else, he'd sleep.

I kept edging away.

I was aware, from the corner of my eye, that a patrol car was creeping slowly down the streets. Lights off.

Lynch either did not notice, though, or he did not care. He

gave me a curious look, and I thought for just a moment that we had connected, that he understood what I was saying.

His lips pulled back, showing his teeth, and the glaze clouded his eyes. We had not connected after all. He had been studying me like prey. He was hunting me.

And then he was there in a split second, just like Lola had described, right in front of me, grabbing hold and taking me down, swiping at my head like a bear.

"*Noah, god damn it*." Moira was out of the house and on the porch. She fired a shot in the air, running toward us, but Erebus Lynch was too close to take down.

The cops were out of the car, shouting for her to put down her gun, but she didn't. She jumped on his back with a scream, and he let go of me and spun around, the cops running toward us as she hit the ground and Erebus Lynch ran, then faded into the night.

I grabbed her and wrapped my arms around her.

"You're covered in blood . . ." She sobbed.

"Head wounds always bleed, Moira, I'm fine. It was just a scratch. Did he hurt you, are you OK? And you jumping on his back like a cat."

But she laughed. "Next time you tell me to take some guy out, sweetheart, would you please give me enough distance between you to do just that?"

I laughed too.

She touched the side of my face. "He hurt you. You really are bleeding, and it looks like you got punched by a bear."

"I don't know what that looks like, but it *feels* like I got punched by a bear," I admitted. "Some date night, huh?"

"Remember the good old days when we used to go to the movies?"

"Remember the good old days when there was something that we wanted to watch at the movies?" I kissed her hard. "Thank you for running him off."

"I thought he was going to kill you."

"I did too."

The police officer who gave chase came back, panting. "Could not catch him, he just . . . he just disappeared. Is this the guy? The one we've got reports about at the Opera House? The Night of the Living Dead, Phantom of the Opera guy?"

"That's the guy."

He grinned. "You just made my night." He spoke into the radio on his shoulder. "Yeah. It's him." He looked back at me. "You OK? I can call an ambulance."

"He's a doctor," Moira told him. "And by that I mean he will turn down medical care no matter how bad off he is."

I managed to head off the ambulance, but there were forms to fill out before the cop would leave us be. As always.

"I have to say, Katani called this," I said to Moira later. "I tried talking to Erebus. It always looks like he's listening, but what he's really doing is planning how to kill you." We were curled up in bed with a Sriracha barbecue pizza and some of the Ducati bourbon Ray had sent over. "There's no way to get through to him. No way to help him. He's too far gone. But if I'd gotten to him earlier, maybe just as he was starting the regeneration process—"

She held out her glass. "If you're going to talk shop, I need more bourbon to tune you out. I was almost listening there myself."

"Ah. I like how when you drink bourbon you say what is really on your mind, which is something that often baffles me. And now I have the solution. What do you want to talk about?"

"I liked the part where you called me baby doll."

"I liked the part where you jumped on his back."

Early the next morning, when I went into the hospital, I had lost another TBI patient who'd slipped away right before dawn. And Agent Liam Katani was gone too—or rather, his room was empty.

Just to be safe, I went down to the basement and into the morgue. Katani wasn't there, which was a relief. It looked like everyone in there was going to stay dead. Which was something I could no longer take for granted.

THIRTY-SEVEN

Early in the morning, two days later, I was out of the house just as the sun was coming up and heading to my car when I saw the Tahoe pull up in front of the house. I could hear Tash setting up a fuss.

Agent Katani got out of his car and stood by the curb waiting for me.

"Hey," he said.

"Hey."

"You did it, didn't you? Gave me those autoimmune meds after I'd . . ." He hesitated. Looked around. "Fallen asleep?"

"Guilty." I could not stop the smile when I said it. "I have no idea why I'm so damn glad to see you. And you look different somehow. Rejuvenated. Did you have work done? Botox?"

He grinned. "You think my face is pretty, have a look at my hair."

"What have you got tucked under your jacket, Agent Katani?"

He unzipped his jacket halfway down, and a puppy with big eyes, floppy ears and a very large nose peered out.

"Did you or didn't you tell me to get a dog? You were right there when I made the plan, weren't you listening? I decided you were right and I'd give it a shot, starting with this little guy. His name is Shrimp. All according to plan. He's going to be a big dog. I might predict . . . *huge*."

"Where'd you get him?" I asked.

"He found *me*, when I was leaving the hospital. Pardon me for just heading out, I didn't want to explain how I got healthy so fast. The U.S. government will take care of the bill by drowning the admin staff in paperwork until they give up. I was walking past a dumpster and I heard Shrimp crying. I think he was cold. Hungry and cold and lonely. What was such a little baby dog doing out in the world on his own?"

"Waiting for you?"

"So I picked him up and put him in my jacket and he went right to sleep. Puppies know when they're home safe. I took him to the pet store when they opened and he has more stuff than I do now. He's got a tee shirt too. I was actually going to bring him to *you*, but after I got him in that sweater, and fed him Royal Canin kibble for big dog puppies, and we played with his very first ball . . . I knew he was my forever dog."

"Off to a good start, Liam. Call my office, we'll set up your first appointment. Perry and I will make sure you're well—and that you *stay* well."

He nodded. "I'll see how it goes. I'm going to take your advice, Noah. However long he lives, I'm in. Other than that, no promises. Speaking of which—did you and Jesse pick up my phone? I'd like it back."

"Jesse has it. He's probably cleaned the blood off for you."

"Much appreciated. Is the tracker I put on Lynch showing any activity?"

"Not that I know of. Lynch is probably dead, Liam."

"Dude. Probably? You've always got to make sure."

"He's not eating. He's not drinking. Because dysphagia means his muscles aren't working so he can't. And—"

"Noah. Why do you think I have such great hair?"

I stared at him. Puzzled.

"Regeneration is ongoing—not to the extent of coming back to life, but Erebus Lynch is regenerating, building new tissue and neural pathways, and your timeline of how long someone can survive in his condition doesn't apply. Because he *can get better.*"

I thought about that. "Does that mean I can help him?"

"I doubt it. His body might heal, but that doesn't apply to his mind—to his soul. It just means he may live longer than you think. Come back stronger. Come back even more violent—and even more evil. Whatever dark force has him in its grips, they're not going to let go. So, we have to find him. Before he finds us."

THIRTY-EIGHT

Moira was curled cross-legged on the bed, watching me get ready before we went out. I was fresh from the shower, with a towel wrapped around my waist, hair wet and slicked back, shaving.

"Shit." Blood trickled down my shin. I looked over my shoulder at Moira. "Why do you love to watch me shave?"

"I just do." She gave me a worried look. "I watched you out there the other night, in front of our house. He was following *you*. Erebus Lynch. I saw what you did."

"Which is what?"

"Mastered your impulse to be the steady, safe doctor in charge, the man who will heal you and save you, even if it gets him killed."

"Is that sarcasm I hear?"

"Pride. You did good."

Her hair was down and loose, and the sweater she wore slipped off her shoulder, and she left it there, which I found entirely distracting.

"If I'm reading your signals correctly—"

"Sweetheart, don't analyze it. Just do it."

I wiped the last of the shaving cream off my face, then went and sat beside her on the bed. I pulled the sweater off her shoulder. "Are you going to boss me around?"

"You bet I am."

"I love it when you do that."

"How could you not?"

THIRTY-NINE

When the call came through from Perry, Moira and I were having a date night downtown, and I had planned it for romance. We'd dressed up, left the kids with Moira's little brother, Tom, and said we'd meet all of them for brunch late tomorrow morning. Very late.

We'd booked a room right next to the restaurant at the Marriott City Center, which was lit up and buzzing. We had an eight p.m. dinner reservation, and had taken an Uber into town.

There was no better place than downtown Lexington on a Saturday night. Lights strung up and down the streets, upscale restaurants, modern high-rise apartments amidst the Art Deco and Italianate buildings that had been renovated and gave the city an elegant charm. Sidewalks thick with people laughing and full of energy, and happy just to be out for the night. A lot of them young.

We dined at the glitzy, Art Deco Jeff Ruby's Steakhouse. It was the kind of restaurant that had a dress code and a menu of after-dinner cigars. The service was gracious and warm, and the interior was right out of the Gilded Age with Keeneland racetrack and thoroughbred horses as a theme. We sat in a horseshoe-shaped red leather upholstered booth, and decided if we came back again, we'd sit on the patio outside.

I had the bourbon fillet, with chive potato purée, bourbon garlic shrimp and crispy onions, and a side of grilled asparagus. I had considered the lobster gnocchi but wanted to leave room for dessert. Moira had the steak Diane, with mushrooms and brandy cream, and the baked macaroni and cheese. We split an order of bananas Foster, with coffee. We passed on the Rémy Martin Louis XIII at $285 per ounce, and were content with Courvoisier.

Afterward, we walked hand in hand down Vine Street. We were dressed up, feeling light and happy with the wine, the night air, each other.

Then my phone rang.

"Dammit to hell." I looked up at Moira. "It's Perry. I have to answer."

She nodded, and pulled away from me, settling on the side of a fountain.

I wasn't having it. I sat close enough to crowd her, and had to grab her before she fell in, and she laughed and I held her hand tight so she could not get away.

"Perry, I have you on speaker phone so Moira can hear you, because we are having a date night. So if it's not an emergency—"

"It is."

"Call 911."

"I did. I just heard from Jesse. The tracker Liam had on Erebus Lynch just went live again; he's on the move."

"Shit." Liam called it once again, I thought.

"Jesse's in a panic. Erebus is on Main Street, he just turned down Vine."

"Shit. We're on Vine," I said, and Moira and I both craned our necks, looking up and down the street. If Erebus was here, he was keeping a low profile. For once. No one seemed alarmed. No one was screaming. "Where do you think he's headed?"

"Ray and Lavee are having a small celebration for her birthday at the rooftop bar of the Marriott City Center. They do it every year, it's always for family and friends, but Jesse and Lola refused to go tonight. Jesse told me he was shocked to learn they weren't planning to cancel."

These things are hard on kids even when they're grown. Parents having lives.

I took another look down the street. Still no sign of Erebus. "I think we let the police handle it. You said they're on the way. Tell Jesse to call his mom and warn her."

"Jesse can't get her on the phone, or Ray either. He's going over to warn them himself, but this could turn into something. Maybe you and I should go to the bar ourselves."

"Just call Katani and tell him to come in the Tahoe with the winch," I said grimacing.

Moira leaned close to the phone. "Hey, Perry. It's Moira.

Noah and I are actually real close to the Marriott, so we'll run up to the rooftop bar and let them know."

"Moira, maybe you should stay—"

"Goodnight, Perry," Moira said, taking my phone. I only just caught her hand before she threw it into the fountain.

She gave me a sideways look. "What's all this about a winch?"

FORTY

When we arrived, Ray was cutting the strawberry and champagne cake from Martine's, and Lavee was handing round plates. Nine people gathered round a few tables, some couples, some not, all holding glasses.

Lavee saw us and smiled. Came over with two glasses of champagne, one she handed to Moira, the other to me. "I'm so glad you and your wife could come."

No one mentioned that we hadn't been invited. This was the south, after all.

Lavee looked stunning. She was wearing that string of pearls she loved, hanging to her waist, a simple black dress, low-heeled strappy sandals, and her hair was tied up in a lush, loose chignon, with wisps of hair curling softly to her shoulders. Dangling pearl earrings completed the ensemble, of course. She was, after all, Lavee Lynch.

Ray was right behind her, elegant in a black tux, and he wore it well, his hair gelled back, thick and wavy, eyes deep set, and the steady watchful presence I was beginning to know. He handed Moira and me plates with slim and elegant slices of cake.

He gave Moira a little bow. "How lovely to meet you, Mrs. Archer. Do me a favor—try that cake right now, and tell me what you think."

It had only taken him three seconds to charm my wife.

He leaned close to me. "Everything OK?"

I imagined he felt the same way I did a few minutes ago when Perry called.

I drew him to one side. "Jesse asked me to stop by," I said, my voice low, so Lavee couldn't overhear.

"Something up?"

I nodded. "It's not over. Erebus Lynch is on the move again. Katani has a tracker on him, and he's headed this way. Jesse wanted me to warn you."

"I see," Ray said, eyes going hooded and dark.

"The police are on the way too."

He sighed. "God knows how that will go. By the way, I've finally let go of the storage unit. The Caddy is now crushed into a block. And I managed to convince my wife to quit laundering her dead husband's shirts."

"I always admire the way you get things done."

"I'll be on the alert, but I'm not going to tell Lavee. It's her birthday. I'm officially giving her the night off from Erebus Lynch. I'm beginning to think I could google him and he'd come up under the category 'Your Worst Nightmare'. I suppose it's too much to ask to have one night off from this kind of thing." He stopped, looked back at me over his shoulder, giving Moira and me a second look. Smiled. "Please know that I am glad to see you, whatever your news."

"Why don't you shut the party down, Ray, and get everybody out?"

"How long before Erebus gets here?"

"Any minute now."

"Then there's no time. I'd rather keep everybody together up here than have them in the elevators and out on the street looking for their cars. Better if the police get him contained before he arrives."

The sound of sirens and flashing lights sent us out through the open doors, to the deck and the rooftop pool. Ray and I stood side by side, looking down.

He sighed. "Let's hope they get him. I would appreciate it if you'd stay, though, Dr. Archer. Just in case you are needed. In the meantime, I promised my wife a dance."

Moira was sitting at the bar eating cake when I went back inside.

"I heard sirens," she said.

I nodded. "If we're lucky, they'll grab him outside the hotel."

She fed me a bite. The icing was thick and not too sweet, the cake in thin pink layers with hints of strawberry and champagne. I set my glass down on the bar and she ate the full slice of cake on my plate, while I finished the crumbs left on hers.

"Why are we still here?" she said.

"Anything could happen, Moira. I can't leave them with this. Erebus Lynch is still dangerous, even now. Maybe even more so if Liam's speculations are right. Speaking of which, why don't you go check in and—"

"Not a chance," she said. "Somebody's got to protect you."

"True. I'll be your backup."

She drained the last of her champagne. "If he's really coming to terrorize and kill us all, it would be convenient if he got on with it."

I heard tapping on a champagne glass. Ray was smiling as soon as he had everyone's attention. "A toast. Happy birthday to my wife, Lavee Lynch, the woman I love most in this world, and have since I fell in love with her when I was a bad, wild, high-school dropout at fifteen years old."

She touched his cheek and smiled.

That's when the music started. Josh Turner singing "Your Man".

"This one's for us, Lavee. Let's get a dance in while we can."

Ray took Lavee's hand. We lifted our glasses and drank champagne in a toast to the happy couple, and I noticed that although Ray was still smiling, he was now watching the hallway and his eyes were hard.

Lavee froze, looking back over his shoulder with a big smile. The door to the stairwell was open and Jesse was bounding through. In his best jeans and boots, hair slicked back, and he was running toward us, looking straight at his mom.

"Jesse, you're not supposed to be here," she said, surprise and delight warring with suspicion in her voice.

"You invited me." He laughed and gave her a quick kiss on the cheek.

"Lola OK?"

"She's fine. She told me to wish you happy birthday."

"She really did?" Lavee asked.

"She really did. She also said for me to show you this. The latest ultrasound scan of your granddaughters. We heard the heartbeats. The girls are happy and healthy, despite everything."

Lavee took the picture, and I saw the glow of happiness and relief in her expression. She caught my eye and we exchanged a look. Things were going to work out, after all.

"We're going to name them Lavinia the Second and Raylene."

Lavee laughed. "You better not."

Jesse took both her hands and gave her a steady look. "I love you, my beautiful mama. And I'm sorry, but no more dancing for you tonight. Ray, get her the hell out of here. Dad is on the way and he's coming for her. Katani is tracking him with an AirTag, and he's right on the corner of Main Street and Vine. He was still for a while, but then he started moving. ETA three minutes. Katani and Perry are in the elevator coming up. Katani has a Taser and restraints, but I wanted to get here fast to give my mama a kiss. Now go. *Please*. This is my problem now."

"You don't look scared," Lavee said.

She was right. Jesse did not look the least bit scared. He looked upbeat and psyched and he smiled at his mom. "Come on, Mama. Let me take care of this once and for all."

I figured that meant Katani had come with the winch.

I wondered what it meant for me that I was happy about that now.

The elevator right outside the bar dinged and the door slid open.

A woman in the hallway began to scream.

FORTY-ONE

And there he was, Erebus Lynch. Yet again. If he saw me, he didn't care. He had eyes only for Lavinia Lynch, and I could only be grateful that Lola had not come. She and her precious cargo were safe, even if the rest of us were not.

And then things happened very, very fast.

First the soundtrack, preprogrammed to make Lavinia Lynch happy, switched to Louis Armstrong singing "What a Wonderful World".

For a moment, just for one split second, everyone in the room was frozen. Shock. There wasn't a person there who did not know who Erebus Lynch was, that he had somehow come back from the dead. The whole damn city knew and they were buying tickets to see him at the Opera House, full to capacity every night. But that did not mean they had truly believed it. Not until the man himself—the monster—was right in front of their eyes.

Everyone froze but me. Lynch was blocking the exit and I needed to get Moira out.

"Behind the bar," I said.

Moira wasn't frozen either, as it turned out. She ignored me and grabbed the cake knife.

Erebus Lynch seemed to be fighting against the music, bobbing his head like he was trying to shake it off. He broke free of his paralysis, then made a beeline for Lavee.

The monster's muscles were twitching and jerking as he lurched forward at a speed that didn't seem humanly possible, moving with a leg-swinging stride that I knew from experience was his way of staying in balance.

Liam had been right yet again. Lynch's body was regenerating. He was faster, stronger, more vicious than ever, even as his mind slipped further away from anything resembling sanity. And we were right in his way.

Lynch went straight for Lavee, and Ray stepped in front of her in an effort to protect her. But Lynch was in the red zone now. And I thought of the pictures that Liam Katani had shown me, and how we had casually talked about animal attacks, and how brutal Katani had seemed. The damn winch that had got me so upset with his unkindness. His brutality. But now I understood.

The violence of him. The strength. The wild, lethal look in his eyes. Whatever had made me think this man could be contained?

It happened so fast. The blood, the screams, the guttural cry of pain. Not believing what I was seeing with my own eyes. Ray torn apart, falling to the floor, in a river of blood and viscera and bone fragments, mouth open in a snarl, which was all that was left of his face.

Lynch turned to Lavee. She backed away, but held his eyes, and he was mesmerized as she began to sing. "Moon River". Maybe she thought it would calm him. How pretty she looked, I thought, frozen with horror, my mind working as I ran through plans that wouldn't work, Moira grimly clinging on to my arm to hold me back. All I could do was pray that Agent Katani would arrive soon, that Lavee could hold off the man who'd once been her husband for long enough.

All fixed up for her birthday party, in a spaghetti-strapped, below-the-knee silky black dress, mahogany hair escaping from that masterful and loose chignon, Lavee looked so sophisticated. So pretty. And so, so afraid.

But also . . . resigned.

Because she had always known this would happen. Women married to men like Erebus Lynch always know that eventually, they'll get taken down. What everyone else believed to be unimaginable was always her everyday life.

I couldn't just stand there and let it happen. I took the knife from Moira, who sobbed, and I targeted the hamstrings at the back of his right thigh, hoping to bring him down. The blood gushed juicy and red as I went in for a sewing-machine attack, striking again and again, slicing all four quads and catching the iliopsoas muscle as well. I'm a surgeon; this is what I do.

He staggered, his leg buckling, but he stayed on his feet and kept his focus on her.

It was a lovely night. Warm with just a hint of breeze, and the outdoor section in front of the infinity pool had been opened up, with chairs and tables and patio lights and a view of the city. Lexington, so beautifully lit up, teeming with people out to have a fun night, restaurants, the Opera House, hotels, Rupp Arena, high-rise apartments, wide sidewalks, Triangle Park with the fountains that were lit up at night. Where the ice-skating rink was set up at Christmas, where my children went to watch Disney on Ice.

Comic-Con was on for the weekend, and the sidewalks were full of people in costume, light sabers, full of energy and the thrill of a convention of heroes, plastic bags full of trophies and souvenirs hanging from their arms.

And they screamed and froze, down on the sidewalk, looking up when Erebus Lynch lifted Lavee in his arms and threw her from the rooftop bar of the Marriott City Center to the street below.

Whose screams I heard were hard to sort. Some were my own.

Lavinia's arms flailed as her silky dress whipped around her legs, and it seemed to take so long for her to fall. And then she hit the ground and died and the blood pooled around her on the concrete sidewalk below.

Jesse cried out, but Erebus Lynch was not done. He lurched across the room, limping hard and bleeding out but still on his feet, and I knew he was heading straight for his son.

I heard the elevator door open again, to Agent Liam Katani, the Lucky Hunter, come to bag Erebus Lynch. Katani knew what to do. He'd done it countless times before. He'd told us that the families of regenerates were always glad to see him. I didn't believe him then. I believed him now.

The Taser hadn't worked before, so Katani hit Erebus with something new, a high-powered tranquilizer dart, a massive dose of xylazine and Carfentanil, enough to bring down a water buffalo.

Lynch staggered and kept on going and I saw the shock on Katani's face. This kind of near-total cognitive decline and psychosis meant that his body would suffer the pain, but the drug did not shut him down; tranqs were never a sure thing.

Katani shocked him twice with the Taser before Lynch reached out and grabbed him by the throat.

Katani was good. Really good. And he had grappled with creatures like Lynch before, experienced hunter that he was. But now Lynch had him tight by the throat. Katani knew it was hopeless . . . and so did I.

But we hadn't factored in Jesse.

"Dad."

Erebus turned, letting Katani go.

Jesse was a by-God streetfighter and he moved fast. The switchblade knife was out of the pocket of his jeans before I could blink, and I saw the flash of a narrow six-inch blade. It was designed for killing. No serrated blade, no angled point to make it catch on bone or sinew, just sharply honed and ready for business.

Jesse stabbed his father fast and deep three times, spatters of blood darkening the even tan of his face.

Erebus Lynch wailed in pain-filled rage and went down hard, twitching as he bled out on the floor of the rooftop bar.

Jesse put the knife back in his pocket when the thing in the shape of his father stopped moving, looking down at him. "Bad Dad Tango. Burn in hell, you son of a bitch."

Katani was back up on his feet. "Jesse," he said. "Go now with Perry to the NGO office on Manchester. Don't talk to anybody and wait for us there. Noah and I will join you both as soon as we can."

He turned and raised his eyebrows at me, and I nodded. I knew what he was asking, and I was all in. Even if it involved a winch.

"What are you going to do?" Jesse asked him.

"Keep your ass out of jail. Give me the knife. That definitely isn't legal. But Ray bought it for you, right?"

"Hell yeah, it was a gift from Ray. He taught me how to use it, too."

Katani nodded. "Believe me, I'm impressed. And thankful. But right now I'm going to have to handle things here, which means dealing with first the cops—and then your father's body. Noah and I have to make sure that he'll never come back."

FORTY-TWO

I took a moment to kiss my wife goodbye and walk her downstairs to the Uber. She was trembling softly, and I put my arm around her.

"I don't like just putting you in a car and sending you home on your own," I said.

"I'll be OK. OK enough, at least. How about you? Looks like you have a hellish night ahead of you."

"It's righteous. I have to make sure Lynch does not come back. Please know, though, that I am in awe of how lethal you looked with that cake knife, and will keep that memory close for the rest of the night. Maybe the rest of my life."

"Did you see me lick the icing off?" She gave me a shaky laugh. Kissed me goodbye. "We're still alive," she said, and smiled.

"So we are."

She cupped my face with both hands. "Remember. You cannot heal him; you cannot help him. Make sure he is dead and gone and nothing but ashes by the end of the night.

I nodded. There is nothing like a woman for moral clarity. She kissed me hard and was gone.

I was three steps away when I heard her call my name. I turned around. But it was not Moira who had called for me.

A woman was suddenly standing beside me, as if out of nowhere. Robust and round with dark lush hair pinned up and falling down around her shoulders. She wore a heavy black skirt, calf length, with a white button-down shirt tucked in tight, and very practical barn boots on her feet. I felt her hand on my shoulder.

"Hello, Noah."

I looked up. "Hello, Maudie. Not to be rude, but say what you need to say. I've got a monster to get rid of. And I don't want to leave your great-grandson alone."

"I am so grateful to you, Noah. Liam is heading in the right direction, thanks to you. The rest is up to him now, though anytime you want to lend a hand, don't hold back."

"Yeah, because Liam is easy to lend a hand to."

The smile she gave me was gentle and concerned. "I promised to return the favor, Noah. So let me tell you this. You have made a choice to kill Erebus Lynch. You who saved my great-grandson. And doing that will keep those babies safe, keep Lola and Jesse safe, and they will have their future. I wish it wasn't this way, but it will come at a cost to you, down the line. It's the right thing, to warn you."

"I'm not backing down," I told her. "I can't think of anything worse than letting Erebus Lynch get away with this. He has to be stopped. No matter what."

"It's the no matter what that worries me, Noah. But you've made the proper choice. The brave choice. Because of the man you are. If you do this, you'll never completely be rid of Erebus Lynch."

"It will haunt me forever if I don't."

She nodded. "I know you want to find a way to make it good for all of them, but Erebus Lynch already made choices, and he is barely there. The darkness inside him is what he feeds on now, as it feeds on him. As it will feed on you."

"Don't you think that if I can raise the dead, I can make it safe for all of them?"

"Them? Yes. But not you."

"Next time you get the urge to do me a favor, lady, just don't. And don't waste any time worrying about me. I've been wrestling with the darkness all of my life."

She nodded. "This is the man that you are. Be good to your wife's kitty, Mr. Timothy. He loves your wife. But he belongs to you."

I watched her turn away and fade into the darkness, which was a serious relief. I hoped that I would never see her again. I envied Liam Katani for that head of hair, but he could keep his unsettling great-grandmother. I turned away. I had shit to do.

FORTY-THREE

Katani seemed like a different man as he spoke to the police detectives who had arrived in force on the scene. He showed his badge and then exercised the power of the AARO as defined by the latest presidential executive order. He explained to them, with grim courtesy, that as the death of Erebus Lynch was now a Department of Defense classified investigation, all matters were designated as sensitive and requiring protection against unauthorized disclosure for reasons of national security. He had paperwork in the trunk of his car, regarding the handling of classified information and the rules and procedures for preventing leaks or misuse of information, which he was happy to provide, and did so. Access to the body and the witnesses was now controlled; information would be given on a need-to-know basis, and only to those with the proper high-level security clearance.

He would be taking charge of the remains of Erebus Lynch for reasons of national security. He would release the bodies of Lavee Lynch and her husband Ray to the Fayette County Coroner, to be processed under local regulation. While he could not share any specific UAP data, he wanted to assure them that the AARO would examine Erebus Lynch, and that while it was highly unlikely there would be any evidence of extraterrestrial origin, for reasons of safety and security the UAP would have to run extensive tests and conduct a full autopsy and examination. The investigation would likely take several months, and he apologized for his inability to confirm the timeline at the present moment, assuring them that if his office determined any risk to person or persons on scene, they would be notified at the earliest possible moment to ensure their ability to secure their own personal safety and health.

By that point they were as glad to see us go as we were to leave.

Nevertheless, the techs from the coroner's office reluctantly offered to help move the body, and while Katani turned them down, I thought he was impressed with their professionalism.

Together, Katani and I bundled up Erebus Lynch's body, zipped it up in a black body bag, and maneuvered it into Katani's Tahoe, which was proving to be a most useful vehicle. I wondered what else he had in the trunk of his car, but I really hoped I wouldn't find out.

FORTY-FOUR

The distillery building that contained the Enlightenment Project office space was lit up in the darkness, and restaurants below were busy. The outdoor spaces were full, and nobody gave us a second look. Not even when we hustled the body of Erebus Lynch to the fourth floor and strapped him onto the gurney for an MRI.

He was cold. No twitches, eyes open and unseeing.

We were waiting for Chloe to arrive before I did the MRI. She went straight to Jesse, who was in the corner—Perry had dragged in a chair so he could sit. Jesse was dry eyed and in shock. His arms were folded and he gave his father his unwavering attention, as if he could not bear to think of anything else but seeing this through. But the grief was there. He would not feel it now, but it would be harsh. He'd lost his mother. He'd lost Ray. Lola and the babies would get him through; taking care of them would keep the horrors at a distance. And I saw the smolder of anger. Ray and his mother were gone from him now. But his father, his father was across the room, dead for now, and I knew from the look on his face that Jesse would make sure his father stayed that way.

I would too.

"Noah and I would like to take samples," Chloe told him in a low voice. "Will you give your permission for that?"

He took a breath. Nodded. "Do what you want. What you need to do. Anything you learn will help me later; it could be of help to my daughters. Let him be useful for once in his life."

Katani squeezed Jesse's shoulder then leaned back against the wall, next to Jesse's chair, arms folded, watchful. The puppy was sleeping on a towel on the floor at his feet. He whimpered softly, and Jesse picked him up and kept him in his lap.

“Here’s the plan,’ I said. “I will record my findings, and Chloe, you’ll take the samples. Vital organs, brain tissue, blood. Once that is done, I will give him a lethal injection to make sure he stays dead, and as it is delivered, Perry, I know you will want to give some last words of comfort to Erebus, and try to banish the darkness that holds him.”

“I’d rather do it before the injection.”

“And I’m sorry about that, Perry. Hearing is the last sense to go, so if he has any consciousness, the last thing he hears will be your voice. But I’m not taking any risks. Practicality over compassion. Sorry to overrule you on this.”

Katani nodded. “And then we will take him to be cremated. Twice. I’ve already set it up, and the oven is being heated up and readied as we speak.”

I watched Jesse. His face was like stone.

And so I began.

My findings were recorded as I said them out loud by a hands-free gooseneck microphone, sensitive enough to pick up my voice, and good at eliminating the interference of the noise of electric circuitry. I used the same set-up for surgery, and the familiarity of the tasks at hand calmed me. Steadied me.

Lynch was in cardiac arrest. The cessation of vital function, no heartbeat, no breathing. This is called clinical death and it is based on the outdated and incorrect clinical assumption that cardiac arrest is the end of the line. Chloe, now gloved up, took the physical samples, leaning in close to the microphone recording exactly what she’d taken as she went. Labeling everything and setting it aside to be stored.

Perry looked up at me. “Is it possible he’s in pain?”

“Unlikely, Perry, but I’ve taken care of that, just in case.”

Perry nodded. “Of course you did.”

Death is a process, not a moment. And the process of death can sometimes be reversed, if you can get blood and oxygen circulating through the body.

I was going to make sure that did not happen with Erebus Lynch.

His muscles had relaxed. His jaw dropped, eyelids loose. Skin pale, sagging, bones showing beneath. Malnourished, emaciated, severe dehydration. Pulmonary edema—fluid in the lungs. Normal for the days before death.

At this point a physician would call time of death, a random pronouncement that would take on a gravitas and power it did not deserve. It had been assumed for decades that the brain ceased activity at this point, though in truth, during cardiac arrest the brain was in hyperdrive.

Just like it was for Erebus Lynch.

The MRI was charting brain activity in the hot zone.

Katani was watching me. "What do you see, Noah?"

"I see electrical signals in the part of his brain associated with consciousness. The high-frequency electrical signals are escalating; they're now ten times higher than they were when we brought him in and got him in the machine. His brain waves are . . . his brain waves are synching. The part of the brain that processes conscious experience. Empathy. Memory. The activity just faded, then came back stronger."

"Is this normal?" Jesse said.

I nodded. "These are not unusual results, according to the science of resuscitation and near-death studies. In truth, the brain has intense activity during cardiac arrest. We still don't understand why."

Jesse sighed and settled back in his chair.

Someday when we understand the neurophysiology of death, we will be able to reverse it. Hopefully without the side effects experienced by Erebus Lynch.

What happened to Erebus Lynch defies normal, rational explanation, and is defined in scientific terms as *paranormal*. But in truth it is exactly normal. It is the norm for scientists and academics to come to conclusions that are notoriously beside the point, filtered through the mistaken arrogance of human and male superiority. Their arguments for and against mirror science make the arrogant and common assumption that humans orchestrate the biology of the world. A ridiculous mistake. And a dangerous one.

In truth, by the time we can imagine it, it is already out there somewhere.

It is impossible for me to fathom how many mirror twin

regenerates are out there, if any, or if they will die out before they become a presence and a problem. Liam is collecting data, following up on leads, terrified this future will be his.

I studied the results of the MRI and saw what I had expected. Erebus Lynch's brain showed advanced atrophy of the caudate nucleus and dorsal striatum, which explained the cognitive impairment and violence. The frontal horns of the lateral ventricles—the spinal fluid-filled spaces that cushion and nourish the brain—were significantly enlarged. A sign of aging, as well as neurological and psychiatric issues. It's seen in Alzheimer's, schizophrenia, genetic disorders, brain injuries, and birth defects.

I have seen it more times than I can count, and it always makes me sad.

"It's time, Perry. Are you ready?"

"Noah?" It was Katani. "His left eye just opened."

Jesse groaned and looked away.

I moved to shut the machinery down, but Chloe touched my arm. "Do another MRI. While Perry does the last rites and exorcism."

I nodded.

Erebus Lynch was clinically dead. Heart stopped, not breathing. But his brain was a hive of activity.

You are in there, Erebus Lynch, I thought. Being wracked by the pulses of a brain that does not know what to do. That floods you with emotions that cannot be corralled.

I caught Perry's eye.

"I understand," he said.

I gave Erebus Lynch an injection of the kind of barbiturates used in assisted dying. Watched for physical reactions, signs of distress. Nothing. I have always thought the soul knows when it's ready to go. I wondered if that were true of Erebus Lynch. I wondered if he was ready.

Chloe closed the open eye and positioned Lynch on the gurney, and we hit the control to slide him into the machine.

I looked at Perry. "You've officially got three minutes before you'll be doing an exorcism of a corpse."

He stood beside the table, his voice resonant and compelling. Some of his words familiar. Some of them new.

"I baptize you, Erebus Lynch, into a last and final death, and you will not return. You are not lost. There is always a path for a soul who wants to let go of dark things to make another choice, to find a final way back. You are not trapped. You are not doomed. God will deny you nothing, Erebus Lynch, if you choose to turn away from this hellish evil that lays in wait for vulnerable souls."

Perry put a hand up and his voice grew stronger. "I banish you, dark opportunist, and send you not to the stench of the grave, but to God, who will bring you back into the light. Let Erebus Lynch go; you cannot hide behind him. *You are known and you are seen.*"

The lights in the office went out, and a hot wind began to blow, but the MRI machine was still fired up and recording.

"I call for fortitude," Perry said. "I call for strength. I call for death over evil. You will find no refuge here."

For a moment the room felt like a vacuum. Then the tension began to ease.

The lights flicked back on. The wind and the heat died away. And whatever had been there was gone.

"What did you see?" Chloe asked. Jesse leaned forward, watching me.

I took a breath and let it out slowly. "I saw the extraordinary, Jesse. Your father's frontal cortex was on fire, intense activity that neurotheology associates with spiritual activity. And then everything went quiet. The prefrontal cortex, the frontal lobes, activity in the parietal lobes. It all went quiet."

"What does that mean?" Katani asked.

"It means the area of willful control, of decision-making, relinquished control."

"It means he surrendered to God," Perry said.

Katani folded his arms. "Maybe he did, and maybe he didn't. But the next step is cremation and that doesn't change." He looked over his shoulder. "You with me on this, Jesse?"

"You bet I am."

The puppy stayed deep asleep, safe in Jesse's lap.

It was over.

They all filed out, Chloe murmuring to Perry, and I was left alone. And I was overwhelmed by a wave of such gut-wrenching grief that I had to turn my back and look away from the remains of Erebus Lynch. It hit me hard like a gale-force wind—I was suddenly missing my father and the life I used to have. Nostalgic for the times when I was a boy, coming in hot and dirty from the backyard, Mom in the kitchen, Dad coming through the front door from work, told to clean up and set the table and asked did I do my homework, and our old dog Petey running in behind me barking, and the old television shows, and the way you think it's always going to be forever, and how all of it was so mundane and familiar then, and how I wish so hard I could be there again.

And maybe Erebus Lynch had found peace at last.

But I had no illusions about what would happen to Lynch if he managed to come back. I knew in depth the suffering and the danger he would bring. Katani's great-grandmother had warned me there would be a cost. But this was nothing new. The darkness changes you, it leaves scars on your soul, and a presence that lays in wait for weakness. For me it has ever and always been that way. I knew I had done right by Erebus Lynch, and there would be a price to pay. There is always a price to pay.

One day I too will come to the end, when everyone I love is memory and dust. And I will deal with the darkness then, one last time. And if there is a day that I falter, and step off the path, it will take me then and there.

FORTY-FIVE

Jesse and Perry watched as Katani and I zipped Erebus Lynch back into the thick black body bag, and together we bundled him inside the Tahoe. Chloe gave us a wave and went back into the office, too impatient to wait until morning for results.

It was a good three-hour drive to Harlan County, Kentucky, but in the Tahoe, with Liam behind the wheel, we made it in two and a half. I should have figured him for a lead foot. The thick black body bag containing Erebus Lynch bumped along rhythmically in the back compartment of the car as we headed down the road. By the time we got to Harlan, rigor would have taken hold, the muscles in his body would be hard, and there would be minimal flexibility in the limbs, which would make him easier to handle.

As soon as we hit I-75 south, I felt the surreal thrill of being completely out of the routine of my regular life, speeding down the dark highway, up front in the passenger seat, with the window half down.

I had had a hell of a night. And it wasn't over yet. Not quite.

I dozed as we barreled down the highway into the night, thinking I might tell my sons about this. When they were older. Swear them to silence and leave out the names. I would definitely tell Moira and my brother-in-law, Tom, as soon as I got back.

Harlan County is a beautiful place with lush green mountains. Jeeter's Funeral Home was off Main Street, past the Dollar General store, and a Subway. The sun was up, and I could smell the charred smoky scent of a cremation furnace that had been heating up.

"Better for everyone to stay in the car," Liam said. "Won't take long. Oh, and Jesse, do you want the ashes?"

Jesse shook his head. "I don't think I can face it."

"Keeps it simple." Liam went to the back of the car, opened a metal box, and took out a thick envelope that was clearly full of cash. Business as usual for him. "Keep an eye on Shrimp for me," he told Jesse, handing the puppy into the back seat.

Katani was met at the back door of the funeral home by a guy in his fifties, wearing khakis and a dress shirt. Two young guys in jeans who looked like part-time hires nodded at us. One said "Hey," and they took the body of Erebus Lynch out of the back of the Tahoe, settled it onto a gurney, and disappeared through the back door while Liam handed over the envelope and shook hands with the man, who gave us a wave and headed back inside.

Liam settled back in the car, taking a moment to put Shrimp back in his lap, whistling softly while he started the engine. He made a slow turn onto the street. "I don't know about you guys, but Shrimp needs a wee, and he needs to be fed. I'm starving, and the Subway down the road just opened. Sound good?"

It did.

We sat at a table eating early-morning subs, chips and cookies and drinking Coke, Dr Pepper and orange soda, and it was weirdly normal. Shrimp attacked a half cup of puppy kibble in a bowl. I felt like a college kid again.

Liam ate the last of his meatball sub in one large bite. "So, Jesse, I've worked with these guys before. You've got nothing to worry about. They're good and they're honest."

"They just took an unidentified body without paperwork," Jesse said.

"The good kind of honest, OK? They're here when we need them, right?"

Jesse nodded.

"So they're going to run him through twice, make sure there aren't any fragments. No metal identification either. No death certificate—that costs extra, and you don't need one, right?"

"Right," Jesse said.

"It's over now," Liam said. "Your father's not coming back."

"And may he stay that way forever." He shrugged, gave me a helpless look. "That, Dr. Archer. That was my dad. And now

I get it. Everything my mother always tried to tell me. Now it all makes sense."

Erebus Lynch had never learned that there comes a time in life where you step back from your children so they can get on with their lives. You are always there. Just softly. But Lavee had figured it out just in time.

We did well by Erebus Lynch. We did the best we could.

Jesse fell fast asleep as soon as we headed home, which was too bad. It was a pretty drive back.

FORTY-SIX

It was a relief to be done with Erebus Lynch. A bigger relief to go home.

Tash met me at the door. I could hear the boys playing soccer in the backyard as I headed into the house. Tash followed me, one watchful look over her shoulder, and I felt her soft muzzle as she nudged my hand, then she ran ahead of me just like Petey used to do, and I opened the door, where my wife and my two sons and our fierce and opinionated cat were sleeping and wondered if one day my own sons would look back and feel the same way. I would make sure they had happy, mundane memories just like I do, and I knew to cherish this time with them while I could.

The cat was looking at me. He was at the top of the staircase, where I often sit during the nights when I am worried and cannot sleep. He was waiting for me as he does when he knows I have things on my mind. Cats have never liked me much, but he was softening toward me, as he saw my worth as a co-protector of the family, and I admitted I loved him too. I had never really loved a cat before. I had been missing out.

It was very good to be home.

FORTY-SEVEN

Bad Dad Tango had an extended six-week run, with a new ending. A rooftop moment between father and son, at an extraordinary intersection in the life of one and the death of the other.

I thought of Ray, and the quiet gravitas he had shown that night. Holding Lavee's hand, smiling at her, like a man who might never see her again. He knew what was coming, he knew the risks, but the two of them had made their decision. They would draw Erebus Lynch out one last time. And they would do it out in the open for everyone to see. No more secrets. No more private shame.

The local press was all over it, calling it THE OPERA HOUSE ZOMBIE ATTACK, but in a stroke of pure luck we were not swarmed by the national media, who rarely covered things in the south that happen to *those people.*

FORTY-EIGHT

I was looking out the window of my NGO office when Jesse and Liam arrived together, Jesse on his beloved Ducati, Liam on Ray's vintage Ducati, his little puppy riding along in a baby carrier that Liam had strapped to his chest.

They had asked to meet privately, just the three of us, and I sat in my favorite chair.

I had the results of the tests I had run—the MRIs on Jesse James Lynch and Liam Katani. I had an analysis of what was left of the brain of Erebus Lynch, and I was ready to share my results and my thoughts.

It was late on a Saturday morning, with the sunlight streaming in through the bank of windows, and the buzz of the Saturday distillery crowd below. It was a good energy. I had been to the hospital early, and back in time for brunch with Moira and the boys—and I had stopped off at Martine's for pastries on my way home.

Jesse and Liam were nervous and full of energy in my office, the little puppy running in circles, having a pee on the floor, which I cleaned up. I set out a little bowl of water which he lapped up like champagne, before he peed again. I love them when they're babies.

The days of secrecy were over, the mysteries of Erebus Lynch were unraveling, a mysterious man in life and death. It was all out in the open, and the jokes and snide remarks had been flying fast and furious between Liam and Jesse.

A good thing. To see them take it in stride. To see them realize that this was just a part of their life, not the end of it.

I waited for the fun to die down, an ankle crossed over one knee. There was no hurry. Underneath the jokes, Jesse and Liam were nervous. I would let them play it out.

Eventually the fun died down, and Jesse looked over at me. "Tell me about my dad."

I nodded and went back over my findings.

The brain of Erebus Lynch showed advanced atrophy of the caudate nucleus and dorsal striatum, which explained the cognitive impairment and violence. The frontal horns of the lateral ventricles—ventriculomegaly—are signs of aging, neurological or psychiatric issues. Erebus Lynch had all three.

Neither Jesse nor Liam's brains showed any signs of enlargement—so my conclusion, based on an admittedly small sample, was that the brain injuries had occurred during regeneration, as the zombie cells triggered deterioration as well as regenerated life. The good news and the bad news.

For Jesse and Liam, it meant that they could have a normal life—but they were at high risk of a very abnormal and dangerous afterlife. How they handled it was up to them.

"But I also found increased volume in the parietal lobe. Which controls visual-spatial issues—basically how your brain processes visual information, so this is navigation, getting a feel for distance, recognizing patterns. This is how you create mental images. It's how you find your way around; it allows you to manipulate things, mentally and physically. Which could be an explanation of your father's ability to suddenly go from one place to another as if he just . . . willed himself there. Because maybe he did. Think of it as a higher-order visual-spatial function. On the other hand, it could just be the presence of the possession, which can give you the ability to do impossible, inhuman things. I don't know which it was. Sorry."

"Was there any way . . . any way we could have helped him if we could have gotten him to cooperate?"

I shook my head. "No. Physically, he was too far gone. But the MRI gives me hope. That at the very end there, he was able to let go of whatever held him in that dark and deadly grip."

I explained that my disease progression modeling of Erebus Lynch, based on comparisons of his scan, and the usual trends in the cognitive illnesses I tracked, showed that his brain had hit a trajectory of cascading damage.

"Basically, all I could have done for him was eased the final weeks of his life. Which is a lot. The medical profession has an obsession with cures that ignores the reality that sooner or later all of us die, and a good death is a win. So don't get hung up on cures, guys. Think instead about managing your future."

"So it's all just science?" Jesse said.

Katani laughed. "Right out of *The X-Files*. Our goal—staying dead when we die."

"Or we could come back and be a big hit at Thrillerfest downtown on Halloween. Except, dude, you can't dance," Jesse said.

"And you'll be the zombie doing the tango."

He and Jesse bumped fists.

It was good to see them taking it so well.

Later, when Jesse and Katani were getting ready to head out the door, I looked over at Katani. "So, what are you going to do next? Off to give that winch a workout?"

He grinned. "I'm currently on medical leave from AARO, and I'm going to stretch it out. But I'm tired of traveling . . . I need a home base, so you won't get rid of me that easily. I'll be doing some work with Chloe too. But when I say work, I mean on my database. No more hunting and tracking for me. I just can't do that anymore."

"You saved your little puppy, that's something."

"*It's everything*. But I think he saved me."

FORTY-NINE

In the science of death, more and more people are being revived, people who would certainly have died in days gone by. How is this different? How is this something to kill off and eradicate if it comes with complications, that are not just dangerous to the person who experiences them, but to the rest of us who love them? We are on the verge of great discoveries.

We know so little about what happens after death. We are afraid to know. But what we need to face is that death is not a point . . . it's a process. Death is a phase. To say that consciousness cannot exist after death is a form of ignorance academics cling to. Conflating the workings of the brain, a useful organ for sure, with the consciousness that is who we are, in and above the body.

Consciousness is an entity that is you.

What happened that night on the rooftop will stay with me forever. The violence, the carnage, death, and the sheer beauty and intrigue of knowing there is so much we don't understand about what happens after we die. The dangers. The possibilities. The pure human fear and unwillingness to see what is real, rather than what we expect.

If I ever doubted that your consciousness is truly who you are, and the brain just another physical organ, albeit a useful one, Erebus Lynch would prove to me beyond any doubt that this was true. We are not our bodies, as useful as they are.

Why did he fight so hard to come back? Wreaking havoc and causing pain?

I am grateful for Perry, who kept us tethered to our humanity. To my training that let me understand and offer help—help that I will give to Jesse and to Liam, if they want it or need it. And grateful for this glimpse into the mystery of a human journey of consciousness, which is just as fraught and dangerous and beautiful on both sides of the divide.

As I watched Jesse and Liam roar off on their bikes together, so young, so many things ahead, it made me smile. But this was not for me. I wanted nothing more than to go home, to swing my sons around, to build a fire in our fireplace. To say hello to Tash and Mr. Timothy, our dog and cat. And to hold tight to Moira while I sleep.

Erebus Lynch never figured it out. He would regenerate, and come back to the life he had always known, still singing "Moon River". Still trying to keep a heavy hand on his son, still trying to get away. Still getting it wrong every time. Entitled in death as he was entitled in life. Never understanding that it's the things that tie us down that are the most precious part of life.